Escaping Fear

Book 5 of The
Ravaged Land Series.

By
Kellee L.
Greene

First Edition January 2017

For My Dad.
I will miss you.

Chapter one.

We made it. It had felt like a dream, but somehow we had made it to our destination. After everything, we finally made it to Michigan.

It had taken us nearly four full days of driving around the state before we found the place we'd been looking for. Our new, perfect home was in Northern Michigan, and it was exactly everything I had hoped it would be.

The house we found was almost the same as the one I had pictured over and over again in my mind. Everything about it just felt like it was meant to be. When we first saw it, we all just knew it was the place.

The house was set on land close to the lake, which meant we could have all the food and fresh water our hearts desired. Well, as long as we could catch fish, but both Penn and Carter were confident it wouldn't be an issue.

We had spent a lot of time driving before we found our sanctuary. In fact, we had almost given up. It had been long days of driving and searching. For a while, it had seemed as though we'd never find the place I pictured when I closed my eyes.

As we drove along the deserted roads we struggled to find gas and knew we'd have to find something soon. And then we did.

The house was on fairly secluded property. There were dead and broken tree limbs that would probably never recover from the storms, but there were also trees that were covered in lush, green leaves.

There was a partial fence that went around the yard. It was broken in places and parts of it were missing. It was far from secure. There wasn't anything that would stop someone from walking onto the property and coming right to the house if they wanted to. Penn and Carter made plans to repair it, but they had to put them off when Carter fell sick days after finding our house.

Carter came down with the same thing that had taken Alice and Sienna. At least he had all the same symptoms. Things were bad. He looked like a ghost lying there and neither Penn nor I thought he was going to make it.

Penn would go out and catch fish, and when he returned I would cook them in the fireplace. We did everything we could to make sure Carter ate and drank something every day. Even when he was too tired to open his mouth.

When he could, he'd force open his pallid eyes and frown, "I'm sorry, Ros. I don't think I'm going to make it."

His voice wasn't filled with the fear of what would happen, he sounded as though he was upset he was letting us down. He wanted to be there for us. Helping had given him a reason to live.

"You're going to be fine," I'd say, not wanting to hear about death or dying. There had been far too much of that as far as I was concerned.

Any time I wasn't getting him water or preparing his fish, I was sitting in the living room with him. I didn't want him to be alone, and maybe I didn't want to be alone either.

Carter slept often, but it wasn't ever a restful sleep. He'd toss and turn, often moaning Alice's name or asking for Sienna. Sometimes his eyes would pop open and I'd swear he was seeing them looking back at him.

"Rest... get better," I whispered while my eyes filled with tears. "Please get better."

Penn busied himself filling any jug or bottle he could find with boiled water from the lake. He started working on a storage area in the basement where he kept everything he collected. I knew he just kept working because it was what he needed to do to keep himself sane.

The moment Carter stopped breathing was the point I really believed my days were numbered. I was sitting on the floor next to the sofa when I noticed. I had become so attuned to his breathing that when it stopped, I noticed immediately.

"Penn," I shouted in a pained voice. He came running up the stairs looking as though he was expecting the worst. I looked at him and I tried to turn Carter over from his side onto his back.

"What is it?" Penn said loudly as he came to my side.

"He's not breathing," I screeched, pleading with my voice for Penn to do something to save him.

Penn swiftly rolled him onto his back and put his ear down against Carter's chest. He listened for a second before he put his mouth over Carter's and attempted to breathe life back into him.

"Come on," I yelled at Carter as though there was something he could do about it. When his chest rose, and he gasped for air, I knew it was Penn that had brought him back. His breathing was shallow and slow, but he was breathing again.

"Carter?" Penn said loudly as he watched his eyes flutter. Penn tapped his cheek repeatedly, "Come on, keep breathing!"

There was a long pause before the next breath, but Carter grabbed my hand with a weak squeeze. "Yes," he mouthed.

"Get him water," I said as I placed my hand on Carter's forehead. I couldn't be sure, but it seemed as though his fever had broken. His skin was damp and clammy but he felt cooler.

Penn splashed water as he hurriedly filled Carter's cup. He handed me the cup as he moved around to help Carter lean forward. I carefully poured the water into his mouth.

Carter pulled back and coughed, spewing little droplets of water down his chin. After he swallowed and caught his breath, he nodded for more.

That night Penn and I took turns sitting with him, watching to make sure he kept breathing. When morning came, his color was back, and he opened his eyes with greater ease. He looked at me as though it had been the first time he'd actually seen me in days.

"Hello," he whispered with a weak smile.

"Hi," I said forcing myself not to cry.

"Death came for me last night," he said in a slow voice that cracked.

I nodded.

"Yeah, I told her to get lost... that I wasn't finished here yet," he said with a slow blink and a half-grin.

I laughed, "Death's a girl?"

"I was surprised too."

After that night, Carter's health improved. Each day was better than the last and eventually he was back to his normal self. Both Penn and I were glad to have him back. Carter had somehow managed to fight off the illness that had taken Alice and Sienna only a short time ago.

Over the next several weeks, Penn and Carter took turns traveling to the closest city to our south. They'd go from place to place gathering whatever they could. Penn wanted to build up our supplies as much as we possibly could before winter.

Some of the stores in the city still had usable goods, which made me think there weren't a whole lot of people trying to survive in Michigan. Penn and Carter didn't only go to stores, though. They worked methodically, going from house to house taking whatever might be of use.

Guns and ammunition were among the hardest things for them to find, but Penn had managed to restock our supplies from what he'd found left behind in a few of the houses. We still didn't have a lot, but we were far better off than we had been when we arrived at our sanctuary.

Any time they went to the city, the first

thing on their list was ammunition. Penn believed it was more important than food or water given the location of our home. And he was probably right, but they rarely found what they needed.

The city to the south of us was a solid two-day walk there and back, which didn't count time spent looking for supplies. When Penn left, he would take a large backpack and fill it with anything and everything he could find. There were so many random items filling our basement it looked like we were hoarders, but the basement was also filled with things that would keep us alive.

We'd been working on our supplies and securing the house for weeks when the weather changed. The sky was always a shade darker and the brisk air was damper.

The seasons had been strange ever since the first big storm took away all of the normal from our lives. Fall was here and none of us knew how long it would be until the snow started to fall.

"Winter will be here before we know it," Penn said pressing his palm against the window. He stepped away and started pacing in front of the fireplace. "We need more wood, food, water… what else?"

"I think we could probably ice fish. Food and water shouldn't be an issue," Carter said with a shrug.

Penn shook his head, "Maybe, but we'll need everything stocked up just in case we can't fish for some reason. I'll leave for town in the morning."

"What? You just got back!" I said crossing

my arms in front of my chest. "You've been here what? Two days?"

Carter looked at me, "I can go... it's not a big deal. It's my turn anyway and I haven't run into any trouble yet." He looked around the room and then knocked on a piece of what looked like wood, but was probably a cheap imitation.

"That's not what I meant. You both spend more time away from here than you do being here. Maybe I should—"

"No way. Not happening," Penn said waving his hand in the air as if shooing away my words before they could even make it to his ears.

I stood up, "Really? Carter just said he's never run into any trouble. If you guys can do it, I can do it too."

"Of course you can," Penn said without looking at me. "But I'm not going to let it happen. It's just easier this way. I've done it multiple times. I know where to go and what to do. It'll be quicker if I go."

It was all just talk. He didn't want me to go because he was afraid of all of the things that could go wrong. I'm sure he didn't think I could handle it the same way they could. He was right about one thing though... he would be quicker. But only because he'd done it before and I hadn't.

"I don't know how many more trips we'll need to squeeze in before the snow covers the ground and we can't go. I'll just go this time, Carter can go next time and after winter I'll train you so you can start going too," Penn said turning back towards the window. It looked like he was already seeing what it would be like when it was covered in several inches of snow.

"Uh, whatever," I mumbled as I walked away from him.

For as long as we'd been at our home, no one had come out this way. There probably wasn't another living soul for miles and miles.

They hadn't run into anyone in the city either. It seemed as though the world up here in Michigan had been abandoned. No one wanted to be here.

That didn't mean we were foolish. HOME was always around. If they weren't somewhere in Michigan now, they would be. They wouldn't leave any stone unturned.

I think I had made this place out to be some kind of safe haven where nothing could touch us, but it wasn't. Nowhere was that safe. There were all kinds of threats out there, but the only one we truly feared was HOME. Every morning we woke up, was the day HOME could finally show up on our doorstep.

Maybe that's why Penn didn't want me going to town… because I had let my guard down. Being in this house had caused me to relax somewhat. He knew I wasn't fully prepared, not that I ever would be.

Our house had a single bedroom which Penn and I shared. The first night we stayed here, Carter had fallen asleep on the sofa, and ever since then these have been our sleeping arrangements. Carter didn't seem to mind and no one ever mentioned changing them.

I wouldn't say it out loud but I felt safer being next to Penn. Carter was plenty capable, but Penn had training and I'd known him longer. It was just different.

All three of us usually went to bed at the same time… when it got too dark to accomplish anything else for the day. We had candles, but we rationed them. Each night we kept a small one lit so that if any of us woke, we'd be able to see our way around.

We had flashlights, but those we used less frequently, hoping to save the batteries. But we all knew they'd probably lose their charge over time.

The house had a working fireplace, but we hadn't used it since Carter got well. We cooked our food in a fire pit out back rather than worrying about the fireplace.

There were only so many blankets we could use to stay warm. Once the weather got colder, we'd have to start using the fireplace more often. Penn wanted to save up as much wood as possible until that happened. He and Carter worked on building a woodpile that would hopefully see us through winter.

It wouldn't matter how much wood, food or anything else we had, Penn wouldn't ever think it was enough. We probably had more than anyone else that was still out there… if anyone else was still out there.

When I woke the next morning, Penn wasn't in bed. I put my hand down on his side of the bed but the sheets were cool. He'd been gone awhile.

12

I wished he would have said goodbye, but he rarely did when he went out on runs. The only time he did was if I just happened to be up first, which was practically never.

I walked into the living room and Carter was lying on the sofa with his eyes wide open. The coolness of the living room made me shiver.

"Did Penn leave?" I asked, even though I already knew the answer.

"Indeed."

"Did he wake you?"

Carter sniffed, "Not on purpose."

"Why does he do that?" I said as I dragged my feet along the carpet making my way to the kitchen. I slid an already opened box of granola bars towards me.

"I have a few guesses," he said raising an eyebrow.

"Oh really? And what—"

"Shh!" Carter said his body bolting upright. He waved at me to move down towards the ground.

I followed his order based solely on the urgent look on his face. My eyes shifted up towards my half-eaten granola bar sitting on the counter. I stayed low behind the counter moving slightly to the side so I could see what Carter was doing.

He took several quick, silent steps towards the door and checked the lock. I wasn't sure what he had heard, but he was taking it seriously.

Carter pressed his back against the wall and locked eyes with me. I soundlessly clamped my hand down over my mouth when I saw a shadow

13

slowly creep past the window next to him.

The only thing that separated Carter and the person lurking outside our sanctuary was a thin wood wall. My eyes were so wide I was sure Carter must have realized I saw something. His body was so still he looked like he had turned into a statue.

I pulled my gun, which thankfully I had remembered to grab off of the nightstand and tuck in my waistband. There had been several mornings I'd forgotten it there most of the day. I was lucky today wasn't one of those days.

After several minutes, Carter lowered himself down to the ground. He pulled out his gun and gripped it tightly as he stared at the side window.

Carter held up his palm to indicate he wanted to me stay in the kitchen. Which was perfectly fine with me, since I had no intention of coming out of my hiding spot.

He glanced at the window and then took a deep breath before he launched himself forward and sprinted across the room. I watched as his body moved so fast it looked as though he floated across the floor.

"I saw one," he whispered. "Brown coat?"

I nodded once, "One with a brown coat." But just because we had only seen one, that didn't mean there weren't others out there.

"I need to—"

Knock. Knock.

It was just two short knocks. There was no urgency or desperation. They seemed like normal, friendly, howdy neighbor kind of knocks.

Carter's eyebrows were squeezed together looking just as confused by the knock as I had been. We waited for more knocks but there wasn't anything. No one tried to open the door... no noises, nothing.

That was until there was a squeak against the window. I peeked around the corner at the same time someone cupped their hands around their eyes and tried to peer inside.

I pulled Carter back quickly to make sure we were both well hidden behind the lower kitchen cabinets. Was the candle still burning? Did the house look as though it had been lived in? What would they do if they recognized signs of life?

When the guy knocked on the glass window, I nearly the screamed. But instead, I pressed my lips together tightly and gripped my gun so hard my knuckles turned white.

"Anyone in there?" the voice called through the glass. "Hello?"

Chapter two.

Carter dropped himself down to the ground, so he was laying on his stomach. He stayed out of view but kept his gun pointed towards the door.

"He's leaving," Carter whispered as he crawled military-style towards the window. I followed behind him copying his movements, although I moved much slower.

We both pressed our backs against the front door, neither of us had the courage to look out of the window next to us. Carter was closest to the window that the stranger had looked inside of and knocked on. He gestured, trying to encourage me to look out the window beside me.

I shook my head side to side afraid to do it, but then I threw my hand up in the air and rolled my eyes. Someone had to do it or we wouldn't know if he was still here. I took a deep breath and slowly moved my body upwards. I keep myself as tight to the wall as I could, sliding upward until I was able to look out of the window with one eye.

The stranger was walking away from the house. He was alone, but he moved his head around as though he was looking for something, or maybe someone.

"He's leaving," I said and Carter quickly half-stood so he could peer out his window.

"Huh. Odd," he said as we both watched

the man calmly leave our property.

"Odd in what way?"

"The way he looked around like that. Almost seemed like he was lost or something," Carter said glancing at me as he shrugged.

"Everyone is lost these days," I mumbled, but he was right. It had seemed as though the man was lost or looking for something. But all I really cared about was that he was leaving. Then again, we had let him leave which meant he could come back.

The stranger glanced back at the house one last time before he turned and disappeared through the trees. I turned to Carter, but he was still staring out of the window. He was probably worried the man would turn around and come back and maybe bring others.

I was pretty sure we hadn't handled the situation the way Penn would have. There probably was no way he'd let the man walk away as easily as we had.

After several minutes, Carter stepped away from me and started closing all of the curtains. His words blended into one another, "I think we should keep these closed."

"I think Penn likes them open. To have the upper-hand."

"He's not wrong about much, I'll give him that, but I think he's wrong about keeping them open," Carter said as he walked back towards the window by the door and looked out between the thick, striped fabric.

"I don't know… we can see when people

are approaching. We can be ready for them."

"Like we were this time?"

I tilted my head to the side, but I couldn't think of what to say. He was right. We hadn't seen the man coming.

"But if we close the curtains and he comes back, he'll know we're in here," I said biting my fingernail.

"If he comes back it'll be because he already suspects someone is here. I don't know, let's talk about it when Penn gets back. Until then, let's keep them closed," Carter said letting go of the curtain and walking over to the sofa. He sat down, but he leaned forward resting his wrist on his knees. He didn't bother to tuck his gun back into his waistband.

Carter and I didn't talk much the rest of the day. It was as though we were both afraid if we spoke someone out there might hear us. Or maybe it was because if we weren't absolutely silent we wouldn't hear if someone approached again.

I played solitaire at the table with an old pack of faded, bent-up cards while Carter read a book. I was pretty sure he didn't turned a page the whole time, however. He was too busy looking up at the door every few minutes to concentrate on the words.

When night came, I didn't want to go into the bedroom alone. I was worried the stranger would come back and take us by surprise.

Carter had checked the locks on the doors and windows multiple times. He was feeling just as uneasy as I was and that didn't help me feel better about any of it.

If anyone would have tried to break in, I was pretty sure we would have heard them, but I didn't know if either of us would have enough time to react. Would we be able to protect ourselves long enough so that we could escape? I really didn't want to find out, and I didn't want to be alone in the bedroom if it happened.

"Well, good night," I said looking at the door and then at Carter. There was a small part of me that was hoping he'd offer to stay in the bedroom with me, but he didn't and I didn't ask.

"Good night," he said as he walked over to check the door for the billionth time. It was still locked.

I was just as paranoid. When I went into the bedroom, I checked to make sure the window was locked even though none of us had ever opened it. I readjusted the curtains to make sure not even a sliver of the room would be exposed to someone trying to look in from the outside.

The bed creaked as I lay down on top of the covers. I couldn't close my eyes. My mind wouldn't let me. I stared at the curtain watching for shadows until my eyelids became too heavy and I couldn't stop them from closing.

* * *

The next two days Carter and I spent watching for the stranger to return. Which he didn't. The only movement outside was the occasional bird and, eventually, Penn.

My heart jumped for a second when I saw Penn climb the broken fence and make his way towards the house. I was both happy and relieved to see him.

"Penn's home," I announced as I unlocked the door.

"About time," Carter said as he sat up straight on the sofa and stared at the door. It wasn't like Penn's trip had taken longer than any other time he'd gone out to gather supplies, this time only felt longer because of what happened.

I yanked the door open and smiled at him as he walked past me. He narrowed his eyes at me but then smiled back, "Wow, what a welcome. A guy could really get used to this."

He slowly lowered the stuffed backpack to the ground with a groan. Penn turned to face me. Something about my expression made him look back and forth between Carter and me as though he could tell something was up. But he didn't ask. He closed his eyes and let out a huge yawn.

"Tired?"

Penn barely moved his head when he nodded, "Never sleep good when I'm out there."

"Looks like you got a pretty heavy load?" I asked as I nodded towards the backpack on the ground. It seemed as though I would have a lot to sort through.

"Yeah, it was a good run I suppose. My back is killing me," he said grinding his knuckles into his lower back.

"Old man," I said nudging him lightly with my elbow.

Penn flashed me a half-smile before stepping away towards the kitchen. He didn't make it more than halfway before Carter stepped out in front of him and blocked his way. He looked right into Penn's eyes, "We have to talk."

"About what?" Penn said trying to step to the side. He was probably hungry after his adventure.

"Someone was here," Carter said.

Penn stopped and turned back at me as if he wanted me to verify what Carter had said was true. I nodded, and he turned back to face Carter.

"What exactly do you mean someone was here?" Penn asked as he ran his thumbs over the tops of his fingers.

"Someone was on our property. They snooped around awhile, looked in the house and then left." Carter ran his hand through his hair. I could tell by the slight shaking of his fingers that even thinking about it was making him nervous.

"Is that why the curtains are closed?"

I nodded. "They walked right up without being noticed. Never even saw them coming, so we decided to close them."

"How many were there?" Penn asked as he opened and closed his hand into a tight fist.

Carter shifted his weight and rubbed his elbow, "Just one."

"One that we saw," I added.

"Male? Female?"

Carter answered quickly, "Male."

21

"Did it look like he was from HOME?" Penn asked looking back at me when Carter shrugged.

I shook my head, "I don't think so, but I can't say for sure."

"We need to do something to make sure that this doesn't happen again," Carter said as he walked over to the window. He looked outside for a moment before checking to make sure the front door was locked.

Penn took in a long, deep breath before walking into the kitchen. He started snacking on a granola bar. When he finished it in three bites, he poured himself a cup of water. I could tell by the look on his face that he was trying to come up with a plan to prevent this from happening.

"Hmm... traps, maybe. And we have to work on that fence. It won't stop them, but it'll help slow them," he said opening a second package and taking a huge bite.

"What kind of traps?" I asked crossing my arms and leaning back against the wall.

"Trip wires, nets, pits, anything we can come up with... ideally something that will alert us when someone steps onto the property," he said finishing a second cup of water in one big drink.

I sat down next to Carter on the sofa and watched Penn. It seemed like he was already planning what he was going to do and where he would put all the traps.

"I'll probably fall into one of the pits," I said only half-joking.

Penn chuckled but rubbed his chin while he

looked at me, "Maybe we pass on the pits. We'll start tomorrow."

Carter nodded, but he didn't seem to relax. He hadn't really known what HOME was like, yet he seemed concerned. I couldn't help but wonder if he was worried about more than just HOME coming here. Maybe he was worried about the resistance, or other groups that might be out there trying to stake their claim. Even just a random crazy person could cause problems or be a threat.

Later that night, I couldn't fall asleep because Penn kept tossing and turning. "I thought you were tired?"

"Can't sleep," he whispered. I could hear Carter breathing heavily in the other room. It was obvious that he was already asleep.

"Why not?"

Penn groaned and rolled over onto his side so he could face me. When our eyes met, it made me think back to our time in HOME. I'd slept in Penn's bed so I could get rest... now here I was with him again just so I could sleep. Only he wasn't sleeping.

"The guy who was here... did you see what he looked like?" Penn asked keeping his voice down. He was being careful not to wake Carter.

"I didn't get a good look. He wore a big brown coat with a hood." I closed my eyes trying to picture him, "His face was mostly covered." A wave of frustration rippled over me and I frowned. I opened my eyes wishing I could have remembered something useful. Something that would help.

"I keep thinking about what would have happened if it would have been HOME. I'd come back to an empty place or worse. I wouldn't have known what to do with myself," he said shifting his eyes away from mine.

Even though I didn't know exactly what to say, I felt the same. All I had left to live for in this world was Penn and Carter. I grabbed his hand and wrapped both of mine around his.

"If anything ever happens and I know you are still alive, I will never stop looking for you," I said, and he looked up and our eyes locked. He gazed into mine as if trying to make sure I wasn't just saying what he wanted to hear. "Tell me you'll do the same."

I wanted to hear him say it. I wanted to hear the words. If anything ever did happen, thinking he was out there looking for me or waiting for me would give me hope.

"I will never stop looking for you," he said staring into my eyes. "In fact, should anything ever happen, as long as this place is safe, this is where we work towards coming back to. This is our home now. Always fight to get back here. Promise me?"

"I will if you will."

"Always," he said, and I knew he meant it. "Better yet, let's never let anything happen. Things have been good here… until this guy came snooping around anyway."

Even though Penn could have taken that guy out without blinking an eye, he still seemed to be concerned. Maybe even more concerned because the guy was still out there.

Really, the stranger should consider himself lucky to be alive because if Penn had been here, he probably would have taken him out just for stepping foot on our property. Carter and I should have probably done the same.

"Do you think he's OK?" Penn said quietly as he glanced towards the door.

"Carter?"

"Yeah."

I chewed on my cheek as I thought it over. Carter had seemed shaken by the stranger being so close, but he didn't have the same training Penn had. It didn't seem different from how anyone else would have reacted in his shoes. Neither of us knew what to do, other than to hide and wait it out.

"He's fine… I think," I said saying each word slowly. "Why do you ask?"

"Not sure. I'm sure it's fine. Just seemed out of sorts."

I met his eyes again, "I think we are both just really happy to have you back."

Penn sighed, and I wondered if it was because he was tired of being in charge of keeping us all safe. There wasn't anything I could do about it… he was far more skilled than I would ever be. He was the best at what he did for us and it would always be that way.

The only way someone would ever rival his skills was if Penn taught that person himself. And even then, it would have to be someone very special.

Penn looked down at our hands, "If he comes back… you know what we have to do, right?"

I nodded, but wasn't sure if he'd seen me in the mostly dark room. "Hopefully, he won't come back."

"Tomorrow we'll start rigging up some traps."

I tried not to think about what we'd have to do if the stranger came back. Penn would kill him without giving it a second thought, but could I? Could Carter?

We didn't even know anything about the stranger. He could have just been looking for directions.

"OK," I said as my eyelids started to feel heavy. With Penn here I felt safer, which meant I couldn't fight sleep off as easily as I could when he was gone. And I didn't really want to either.

At some point I must have fallen asleep, but I wasn't sure how long I had been out. When Penn woke me I felt alert, as though I hadn't been sleeping at all.

Penn was sitting there on the bed shaking and gasping for air. His hands were groping at his throat as if he was trying to open it.

He hadn't intended to wake me. I wasn't even sure if he knew where he was.

"Penn?" I whispered, lightly placing my hand on his shoulder.

He practically jumped off of the bed and got down on the floor, ducking behind the mattress. I could see his eyes glowing as he peeked over the top of the mattress. The way he looked at me was frightening. It didn't look as though he had any idea who I was.

When he reached behind his back for his gun, I backed away so fast I fell off of the bed. I hit the ground hard. The force caused my head to tip backwards and I hit the closet door with a thud.

I stayed down and hoped he wouldn't find his gun.

Chapter three.

I took several deep breaths before I conjured up the courage to look over the mattress. My eyes landed on Penn's gun on top of the nightstand, but that didn't make me feel any better.

Carter burst into the room, looking towards the window as though he had expected to see it broken and someone inside. When he didn't see anyone besides Penn and me he looked confused.

The only lighting was from the small candle in the other room and the sliver of blue from the moon hanging high in the sky. It filled Penn's wide eyes. I could see the candlelight flickering inside his large, dark pupils.

"What's going on in here?" Carter said, his chest puffed out. He was looking around trying to spot the problem, but all he saw was Penn and me on opposite sides of the room, hiding behind the mattress.

"I'm not sure," I said between quick breaths, "I think he's having a nightmare." I tried to back further away but the closet door behind me rattled sharply as it stopped me from moving any farther.

The noise seemed to startle Penn back to reality. When he looked at me, it seemed as though he recognized me again. He blinked a few times before a look of total confusion washed over his face.

He shook his head, "Why am I on the floor?" His eyes locked with mine, "Why are you on the floor?"

I looked at Carter and then back at Penn. "You don't remember anything?"

"Uh, no," he said rubbing his forehead. "Should I?"

"I think you were dreaming," I said and slowly got up to my feet, but kept my back against the wall. It wasn't that I was afraid of Penn, he wouldn't ever knowingly do anything to harm me, but I was worried about what was happening to him. He just seemed so out of it. "Are you OK?"

"I... I think so," he said slowly standing up. Carter took a step towards him as if to help, but Penn put up his palm to stop him. "Yeah, I'm fine. I'm just really, really tired and kind of confused. I don't think I slept the entire time I was out there."

"Understandable," Carter said, looking at me to make sure I was fine. "Would it help if I stayed up... kept watch?"

Penn shook his head, "I don't think that's necessary. I'll feel better when we have our traps in place. We can't go back to taking shifts... that was just too hard on all of us."

Carter looked towards the front door, "But just for one—"

"Not necessary," Penn said without blinking.

"I don't think there is anything that will ever help any of us feel better as long as HOME is out there," I said, and Carter frowned at me. I

29

shrugged. It was true, even if it hadn't been the best time to say it.

"Everyone back to sleep," Penn ordered as he sat down on the bed. He placed his hand on top of his gun. It looked as though he was considering taking it off of the nightstand, but he laid down and turned over onto his side.

"Just don't shoot me in your sleep," I said with a small, uncomfortable laugh.

Penn groaned, "I would never. Now go back to sleep. Both of you."

Carter looked at me as though he was waiting for me to dismiss him. I bit my fingernail and nodded. When Carter seemed satisfied with the situation, he backed out of the room.

I sat back down on the bed and waited for my breathing and racing heartbeat to return to normal. Carter was noisily working on getting comfortable in the other room.

After I laid back down, I was having a hard time going back to sleep. I turned and watched Penn's sleeping body, hoping that would help.

It was hard to see his face in the darkness, but I could make out the movement of his eyes, wildly darting around under his eyelids. His arms would jerk ever so slightly from time to time as though he was fighting against someone or something. Even when he was asleep, he was fighting.

Eventually his twitching stopped, and he finally looked as though he was resting more peacefully. Shortly after that was probably when I fell asleep.

The next two days we worked on building traps nearly every waking hour, breaking only to eat. Penn instructed us how he wanted the traps built and we followed his instruction to the letter. We used wires and strings connected to various objects so that if someone walked onto our property and tripped a wire, it would make noise.

Penn considered constructing some that could actually harm a person, but then he looked at me and decided against it. I rolled my eyes at him, but at the same time I was kind of relieved.

We had set up ten noisemaking traps around the yard. Penn went around testing them and each one of them worked. Some worked better than others, making a louder noise when triggered, but he seemed satisfied.

I knew he would still be worried they'd fail or that we wouldn't hear them, but having something was better than nothing at all. At least I assumed it was.

"Let's start on the fence," Penn said and Carter nodded.

"What should I do?" I shouted after them.

"Whatever you want to do," Penn shouted back as they disappeared into the garage, presumably to get the tools.

"Thanks! That's very helpful," I shouted back, but if he heard me he ignored me. I liked it better when Penn suggested tasks.

I put my hands on my hips and looked around as though the answer on what to do would present itself. There was always something that needed to be done, but for some reason, I couldn't think of a single one.

After a quick look at the sky to check the time, I figured I'd make the short walk to the lake to work on my fishing skills. If I was lucky, I'd be able to catch us something for dinner.

Even though I still didn't like the taste of fish, I did enjoy having something warm to eat. It was the closest thing to a home cooked meal we could have, and something about that was comforting. And it was also a big change from eating the prepackaged junk we'd become used to.

Carter still foraged for leaves and berries, which I also enjoyed, but he never found enough. Eating the berries would just make me want more of them.

I was getting better at finding plants and herbs, but I was terrible and picking out edible mushrooms. The ones I spotted were always poisonous or Carter wasn't sure about them, so I just stopped looking.

I could hear Penn and Carter hammering away at the broken boards as I walked towards the back of the house to gather the fishing supplies. Every so often it would stop and I could imagine them discussing the project.

The fence was in extremely poor shape. It would take them a long time to fix it, probably months. They'd have to chop down trees or get supplies from the hardware store on a run to keep the project moving along. It wasn't going to be an easy task, but it was an important one.

If they could find a working truck in town, maybe they'd be able to haul supplies back to our place quicker. But it didn't seem likely. The last several times Penn tried a car that had been sitting, he hadn't even been able to get it to start.

I grabbed the fishing pole, the bait Carter had collected and a bucket from the garage. Before I left the house, I checked to make sure I had my gun securely tucked into my waistband… just in case. Hopefully the traps would work. Or better yet, that they wouldn't even be needed.

I walked away from the house on the dirt path that would lead me right to the nearby lake. It wasn't a far walk from the house, but far enough that I wouldn't be able to see Penn or Carter, and they wouldn't be able to see me either.

As I walked up to the lake, the sounds of the waves rushing against the dock and beach drowned out the faint sounds of the hammer. The water splashed over the sides of the dock as I made my way out to the end. I set the bucket upside-down, cast the line out into the water and sat down.

My cheeks prickled at the cool breeze that came off the dirty, blue colored lake. Soon the water would be too cold to clean ourselves in, if it wasn't already.

When I first felt the gentle tug at the line, I thought it was my imagination, but then I felt it again. The end of the fishing rod bent down so far I thought it was going to snap. I smiled at the fish I couldn't see as I twirled my fingers to reel it in.

The fish wasn't putting up much of a fight. I didn't think it was going to be very big, but I didn't care. I was happy to catch something.

I pulled the fish out of the water as its tail

whipped back and forth trying to get free. It looked at me with its black, googley eyes as though it already knew its fate.

"A feisty one, huh?" I said to the silvery-gray fish, but it just opened its mouth before closing it again.

I carefully unhooked the fish and flipped over the bucket so I could drop him inside. He flopped around a bit before he tried to jump out.

"Sorry," I said looking away so I didn't have to watch him struggling. "It has to be this way."

"Nice catch," a voice said, and I spun around so quickly I almost fell off the dock. The owner of the voice reached out to help steady me but I held up my arm to block him.

He took a step back and smiled at me. It was the guy. It wasn't just any guy... it was the stranger that had been snooping around our house. I was sure of it.

I reached back for my gun, but he held up his palm and shook his head, "Now don't go on and do that. That's not necessary, you hear?"

I nodded and froze, but what he didn't know was that I would do it if he took another step towards me. He didn't appear to be armed but I still took a step back to put more distance between us.

I looked around the area to see if anyone was hiding, but it seemed as though he was alone. If he had set off any of the alarms I hadn't heard them, but I'm sure Penn and Carter would have. Since they were nowhere in sight, I had to assume he'd missed every trap, or that Penn and Carter weren't alive anymore.

"Looks like you caught a real good one there," he said peering into the bucket. "What kind is it?"

"I have no idea. Take it if you want it, but then leave me be."

When he took the fish and turned his back to me I'd have to do it. I'd have to take out my gun and pull the trigger. I wouldn't have a choice. It was the only thing I could do to keep us safe.

"Huh. Really? Well, maybe I will." He looked at the fish again. "If you insist?"

I nodded. "By all means."

"Wow. This is really great. Thank you. You live out here all by yourself?" He looked out over the waves and then back at me. Penn and Carter were probably still alive. I took another step away from him. "Whoa, hold on there, I don't want you backing up so far you fall right into the cold water. You'll catch your death in there."

"What do you want?" I blurted out looking around, hoping I'd see Penn and Carter coming to my rescue. But they weren't there.

"Hmm?" He narrowed his eyes at me, "Nothing. I don't see many people."

"How did you get out here?"

He shook his head, "I just walked out onto the dock, just like you did."

"But how did you come to the docks?"

"I just walked along the beach over there. Didn't you see me?" he said with an awkward grin that made me uncomfortable. I reached back for my gun again. I'd feel safer if I had it pointed at him, and I think he'd be more likely to leave. He frowned, "I asked you not to do that."

My hand shook, and I dropped the fishing rod. It fell down on the dock and lodged itself between two slats of wood. Luckily it hadn't fallen right into the lake because it would have been washed away. Penn wouldn't have been thrilled to have to go to town just to find another fishing pole.

"Here, come with me... I have something I want to show you," he said making an attempt at a smile. He didn't even bother with promises of candy or kittens. Something wasn't right about this guy and I needed to get out of here, even if it meant I would have to jump into the cold, dirty lake.

"I'm going to pass," I said with wide eyes.

"No... something tells me you're not," he said and glanced back towards the house. Maybe he had done something to Penn and Carter. I could feel my heel hanging slightly over the edge of the dock. The water behind me crashed up against the wood, splashing and soaking into my pants.

I took a step back... my right foot hovering over the water. I knew if I went in, he wouldn't come after me. Hopefully, he'd run away, but unfortunately he'd still be out there. Or maybe I was wrong and he'd wait on the beach, watching and waiting.

I took a deep breath and leaned back, but I didn't go crashing down into the frigid water. The stranger made several swift moves forward, grabbed my arm and pulled me along the dock towards the shore.

"Penn!" I screamed, but I didn't think he'd hear me. My voice hadn't even come close to being loud enough. I opened my mouth, but the stranger yanked my arm upwards and spun me so I was facing away from him. He removed my gun from my waistband as if it was something he'd done before.

He pushed the barrel sharply between my shoulder blades, "Try screaming again. I dare you."

The stranger maneuvered me around the trees and when he approached the first trap he paused. He stared at the ground and after a few seconds he must have spotted the wire.

"These traps are a really nice touch," he said with a smirk. "Might just be the best I've come across yet. But you didn't set these up, did you?"

"You come across a lot of traps, do you?" I said between clenched teeth.

"Nah, not really. Not much anymore anyway."

When we were past the trap, he moved more quickly. He'd look in every direction as though he expected to be ambushed at any second… and I hoped that he would.

Every time I tripped over anything, a twig, a dead branch, my own feet, he'd get angrier. I started doing it as often as I could, hoping to make it appear as though each stumble was authentic. I needed to do something so I could break away from him before he took me too far away from my house.

It probably wouldn't be too much longer

before Penn and Carter would notice I was gone and come looking for me. The closer I was, the easier it would be for them to find me.

There was a thick branch poking out of the dirt and I made myself trip over it. I stumbled to the ground almost pulling him down with me.

"Oww!" I said as loudly as I could. He looked at me and practically sneered like a wild animal. I had taken my stumbling too far.

His hand was over my mouth before I could even consider uttering another word. It was clear he didn't care what happened to me. He started to roughly drag me through the trees and away from my home. My arms slammed against tree trunks and my feet bounced against the ground over and over again until they felt numb. The stranger had more control over my body than I did.

After five more minutes of walking something frustrated him, perhaps just how hard it was for him to drag me along while I fought to get away. He stopped and grabbed the front of my jacket. He pulled me close so he could look into my eyes.

I wanted to scream at the coldness I saw in his ice-gray eyes, but I couldn't. The nothingness scared me to my core.

His lip curled up into a smirk and then he shoved me into the ground so hard my teeth rattled. He paced back and forth for a few seconds before he dropped his body down on top of mine.

I screamed, but he pushed his hand down against my mouth so hard it felt like my jaw was going to snap. I pleaded with my eyes for him to

38

stop.

A tear leaked out of the corner of my eye. When he noticed, he tilted his head to the side and watched it glide down the side of my face.

He smiled at me.

Panic set in. I was in trouble. Big trouble.

Chapter four.

He wouldn't loosen the pressure on my jaw. I didn't blink. I couldn't blink. Every muscle in my face and neck had tightened. My body was doing whatever it could to hold itself together.

If the man wanted to kill me, he could have. He had my gun. It would take him just seconds to pull the trigger and end it all.

Whatever it was he wanted from me was far worse. It almost felt as though he was the cat and I was the mouse and he was having a grand old time playing with his prey.

The stranger looked at me with his dead eyes. I don't know what he was seeing, but I was pretty sure it wasn't me. His lips curled up slightly at the ends.

I stretched up my leg and tried to kick him, but I was too weak and too slow. He turned around and wiggled his body so he was on top of my legs.

He wasn't worried about my struggling. It didn't even look like he was the least bit concerned that I might get away. There wasn't a doubt in his mind that he had the upper hand.

The stranger shifted his weight and loosened the pressure on my mouth ever so slightly. I don't even remember thinking about it before I reacted. I drew my lips back and bit down as hard as I could on the meaty flesh of his hand.

His head flew back, and he howled out in pain towards the sky. I tried to dig my teeth in deeper but he slid his hand down to my chin and pressed upwards to close my jaw. I could feel his blood running down onto my neck.

Tears streamed out of my eyes, and I knew there wasn't anything I could do. I wanted to spit out the metallic tasting blood but I couldn't open my mouth. If I even tried he would probably break my neck with one quick movement.

The blood was pooling in the back of my throat and I felt as though I was going to choke. I couldn't breathe very easily through my stuffed nose. Even though I tried to fight the urge, the taste in my mouth made me gag.

"I have to give you credit," he said looking at me with his cold eyes. His hand that was holding my jaw shut twitched, and I knew it was because he was in pain from where I had bitten him. "You're a lot tougher than the others."

I twisted my body to the side hoping to break free. If I could knee him between the legs, maybe I could escape, but he was still too strong. He pushed me back down. I had used up too much of my energy.

He pulled back his fist and hit me in the cheek. I blinked several times. Each one lasting longer than the last. It felt as though I was going to go to sleep but I did everything I could to fight it.

Everything around me blurred. His faced moved in and out of focus and then something hit me in the side. I coughed and pain rippled through my entire body. It was hard to breathe.

I don't know when he got off me, but he was standing there looking down at my body as the world slowly spun us around. Something hit me in the side again. Had he just kicked me?

"Stop, please," I moaned, at least I thought I had. Even though I fought it, I faded in and out of the world with each blow.

When he kicked me in the side again, blackness surrounded me completely. It was wrapped around me like a soft, fluffy blanket.

I wasn't feeling the pain from his attacks anymore. My whole body had just turned off. I didn't think I was dead because I could still hear the thuds and cracks of him hitting me over and over again, but then again, maybe I was only dreaming it.

In my haze, I thought I could hear Dean's voice. I tried to tune it in like a radio dial, "Get up, Ros. Get up."

"I can't," I said, and I tried to move my arms and legs but they didn't move. Maybe the stranger had injured me so severely that I was paralyzed. "Why did you leave me?"

He didn't answer. I had thought I'd felt his presence for a moment but if I had, he was gone now and I was all alone with the stranger.

I tried to look through the darkness to find Dean. If I could find him again, maybe he could help me. Somehow I forced myself to blink. I didn't see Dean, instead all I saw was the stranger staring down at me, but then he quickly turned his head to the side.

By the look on his face I was pretty sure

someone was coming. Penn had found me. He was coming for me. It just had to be him. Carter was probably with him and they were here to save me. In a few seconds, I'd hear a gunshot and the stranger's body would drop down to the ground.

I tried to move my lips to call out to them, but I didn't know if they would be able to hear me. The stranger hopped over my body, and it was like the noises of his running were amplified. He was going to get away.

"No," I moaned at the same time I thought I heard a gunshot. I hoped they got him.

My eyes blinked rapidly trying to bring everything into focus. I tried to look in every direction at once, hoping I could spot Penn. Could he see me lying down here? He had to see me, but where was he? I couldn't see him. Why wasn't he here helping me up?

It felt as though I had been lying there for a long time before I saw three people circle around me. None of the faces looking down at me belonged to either Penn or Carter. I didn't know these faces, Penn and Carter hadn't found me, but these three had. For all I knew they'd finish me off.

"Is she alive?" a young boy asked the girl standing next to him.

"I'm not sure." She turned to the other boy, "Gage, check her. Travis, go over there keep watch." A dark-eyed boy dropped down to his knees next to my head and put his face close to mine.

My body felt so cold I couldn't feel my

hands or my feet. I was shivering... couldn't they see my body moving? Surely they could see I was alive.

"She has a pulse, but it's weak," Gage said. I hadn't even felt him touch me. How did he check my pulse without touching me?

The girl crouched down next to me, "Hey, are you OK?"

Her voice was so loud it felt like a hundred pins were being jabbed into my temples. I could feel the tears flood down out of the corners of my eyes. Each one felt like a tiny bit of ice sliding down my face.

"No," I squeaked, and she looked down my body trying to find what was wrong. I tried to keep my eyes on her as she moved up and down my body.

"Does it hurt here?"

"No," I whispered. It didn't hurt but I also couldn't feel where she was touching me.

"How about here? Or here?"

I moved my head side to side. Her touches were so soft I had barely felt them until she moved down towards my side. I gasped for air and winced before I cried out in pain.

"Owww!" I howled, and the girl looked at the boy with dark eyes.

"I barely touched her." I heard her whisper to him.

There was one good thing about the pain. I knew I was alive. I was one hundred percent sure of it.

"Hmm, I think her rib might be broken or

something," she said to the one she had called Gage. "Travis get the bandages," she said over her shoulder. She looked back down at me, looked into my eyes, and spoke clearly, "I'm Wendy. What's your name?"

"I-ah, um." What was my name? Did I have a name? Of course I did, but for some reason I couldn't think of it.

Wendy waited and then looked at Gage nervously. "Do you remember your name?"

"Ros?" I said, not sounding completely sure of myself. The name came to me as if the information from my brain to my lips had been slowed.

"You don't sound so sure," she said with a smile. "Is there anything else broken, Ros?"

I hadn't even known my rib was broken, how would I know if there was anything else broken? She looked me up and down as though she was looking for something to be out of place.

"I'm not sure... I don't think so," I said with a barely noticeable shrug.

"Good."

Wendy carefully moved the hair out of my face. It tugged at my skin as though it had been glued in place with my blood. How much was I bleeding?

She grabbed something that looked like a baby wipe and gently dabbed at my cheeks and forehead. My whole body felt bruised, but for all I knew, maybe something was broken and I'd notice the second I'd try to move.

The boy they'd called Travis appeared and

handed a roll of what looked like some kind of stretchy fabric to Wendy. She took one end and gave the other to Gage. Together they worked to wrap it around my middle.

I cried as Travis lifted me and they wrapped the bandage. Wendy pulled her end tight and secured the bandage in place.

"There. That should help," Wendy said.

I moaned at the tightness around my ribs. It felt like darkness was coming for me again. It was too much.

"Is it too tight?" Wendy said looking at me.

I watched Gage's fingers move along the edges as he checked it, "I don't think so. We're losing her."

"Ros?" I heard the girl's voice trying to reach me through the blackness that was enveloping me. "Ros!"

"We have to get her to the Doc," one of the boys said, but I wasn't sure which one. My eyelids had become too heavy for me to hold open.

Even though my eyes were closed, it still felt as though the world was swirling around, making me dizzy. I didn't want them to take me anywhere. I couldn't let them.

Penn and Carter would be here for me soon. They had to know by now I was gone and they'd come looking. I couldn't let them take me away from here.

If they took me further away, Penn would never find me. How would I get back here in the shape I was in?

Please! Please don't take me anywhere!

Just leave me here, I shouted. But I knew when the voice echoed in my head, that they hadn't heard me. The only one that had heard me was me.

Chapter five.

When I opened my eyes, I couldn't even make a guess at how much time had passed. I didn't know where I was or who I was with.

My head throbbed, and I felt dizzy. I looked around trying to figure out where I was, but I couldn't make sense of the shapes or colors I was seeing. I felt so disoriented, and the motion I was experiencing wasn't helping matters.

My stomach tightened.

I squinted, and overhead I saw tree branches that looked like claws reaching up towards the sky. There weren't any clues as to where I was, but I knew I was still in the woods.

"She's awake," a voice said.

I was in some kind of cart or maybe it was a sled. At least that's what it felt and looked like, although my vision was blurred. My eyelids became heavy and I tried to fight it, but they closed.

"She's out again," said a fading voice. Those were the last words I heard before I was sucked back into the darkness.

When I woke up again, my vision was a bit clearer. I was in a van... a minivan. I was still moving, and it was making my stomach turn... or maybe that was from the beating I had taken.

They were taking me away from Penn and

there wasn't a damn thing I could do about it. But, I had to try something.

"Wait, no!" I said trying to sit up far too fast. I flopped in slow-motion back down towards the seat. Gage leaned over the seat and put a damp cloth down on my forehead.

"You'll be OK," he said with a toothy smile. "You seem to be super tough," he added with a small laugh. "For a minute there we thought you were dead."

I stared at him with a raised eyebrow. Clearly he didn't know me. I was pretty sure no one in my entire life had ever accused me of being super tough.

"Please," I begged, "stop the car. Let me out."

Gage looked up at Wendy and laughed, "Why would we do that? We have a doctor. He can help you. You'll be back on your feet in no time."

"I need to get back," I said but then I stopped myself from saying anything more. I didn't know who these people were… it could be a really bad idea to mention Penn, Carter or where I needed to get back to.

They were helping me, so how bad could they really be? But it was a risk. I didn't know anything about them. They could easily be from HOME.

I'd have to wait until I could escape. What choice did I have? Eventually they'd stop the car. I was pretty sure they weren't going to kill me because they would have done so by now. Or they could have just let the stranger finish the job.

I just had to wait. Which would probably be easy, considering I felt dizzy and disoriented. I wasn't even sure if I could walk. The interior of the van seemed to get darker, daytime would be ending soon, and I wasn't sure how far I'd make it hobbling along on my own in the middle of nowhere.

I drifted in and out as we drove down the road. When I woke again and forced my eyes to stay open, it was night. The van was still moving, although I couldn't even guess as to where we were or which direction we were headed.

"She's up again," the younger one said. I couldn't remember his name, although I was pretty sure they had mentioned it earlier. He was smiling at me, his white teeth sparkling in the darkness.

"How are you feeling?" the girl... Wendy asked.

I sat up slowly, wincing at the pain in my side. My fingertips glided down my face and I could feel small scrapes and crusted blood. At the top of my forehead there was a bandage. What had that man done to me?

I reached for the back of my head and cupped the giant goose egg that seemed to pulse under my touch. My whole body felt as though it had been through a ringer.

"Uh, not great," I groaned. I took a deep breath, but it caused a sharp pain to ripple through my side and squeeze at my lungs. It felt as though I was being stabbed in the chest with thousands of little knives.

"Here, take these," Wendy said handing me two long, oval shaped pills. "It'll help. It's for the pain."

I weakly held out my palm, but I stared at the pills skeptically. What if they were giving me something else? But why would they do that after everything they'd done to help me? It wouldn't make any sense to wait until I woke up to do me harm, but I couldn't trust that they wouldn't either.

Wendy passed me a bottle of water and smiled. I could tell by the look on her face that she knew exactly what I was thinking.

"Read them," she said as she clicked on a flashlight and pointed it at the palm of my hand. Stamped onto both pills was the brand name. It was pretty unlikely they were anything other than what was written on them, so I took the small risk and swallowed the pills down.

Wendy clicked the flashlight off, but she didn't turn around. She kept her eyes glued to me.

"Where are you from?" she said without changing her expression. It didn't matter to me how friendly and casual someone appeared to be, I still wasn't about to tell them my life story.

"Around, I guess. Been everywhere really. You?"

"Also around." She tilted her head to the side and looked down at her fingernails for a second before shifting her eyes back towards me. Wendy sniffed, "So you just travel all around by yourself?"

"Not at first," I said turning to look out the window. This was definitely something I didn't want to talk about. "You guys know a doctor? Where is he?"

"Yeah!" the younger boy said leaning over the back of the seat. "He'll totally help you feel better. He's like so great."

I looked at Wendy, waiting to see if she'd offer more information, but she didn't. It seemed as though she was just as untrusting as I was.

"What kind of doctor is he?" I asked hoping to squeeze out something... anything.

"Not sure," Wendy said staring at the boy. "What happened to the people you were with."

"They didn't make it," I said.

She shook her head, "Sorry to hear that."

The boy leaned forward and drummed his fingers on my seat. He seemed as though he had about four times the energy of anyone else I'd run into since the storms hit.

"What's your name?" I said nodding towards him.

"Travis," he said sticking out his right hand.

I gently shook his hand and smiled back at him, "Weren't you driving before?"

He nodded enthusiastically.

"You don't look old enough to drive," I said through narrowed eyes. Maybe he was just someone that looked young, although everyone else in this world appeared older than they were.

"I'm not, but lucky for me no one cares anymore. No driver's license needed. No police officers to enforce the laws," he said as if he had everything all figured out.

"I suppose you're right on that one. So...

where are we going?" I asked directing my question to Travis.

He glanced at Wendy and out of the corner of my eye I thought I saw her nod. She was in charge of this little group, that seemed to be quite clear.

"We have a place. I think you'll like it," he said still smiling. He really didn't seem like he belonged out here with the rest of us in what was left of the world. He seemed far too happy to be here. I couldn't help but wonder what his story was. It had to be significantly different from what my experience had been.

"What kind of place is it?"

"You'll see," Wendy said turning around to look out the front window. "We'll be there sometime around morning I think. Maybe you should try to get more rest. You too, Travis."

"OK," Travis said and lowered himself down onto the backseat and disappeared from view.

I didn't want to rest. What I wanted to do was stare out of the window and watch for anything that would give me a clue as to where I was. Or something I could use as a landmark to find my way back home.

Once I got away, I would need to do everything I could to get back to Penn and Carter. The more I paid attention to my surroundings the easier it would be, or at least I hoped. If I did get away, it wasn't going to be easy considering I had no idea where I was since we'd been traveling for hours.

The pain relievers had taken the edge off of

the pain and staring into the darkness was enough
to make me feel drowsy. I tried to fight it for as
long as I could, but one blink must have been too
long and when I opened my eyes again, it was
morning.

I pressed my hand to the cool window and
watched as we pulled up to a large brick building.
The tall building looked as though it had once been
a small hospital, a clinic or some kind of institution.

"Here we are," Wendy announced as she
turned to look at me. She watched as though she
was waiting for me to be happy about being in this
strange place, but she was going to wait a long time
if that was what she wanted.

I looked away from her and back towards
the big building. I was trying to find a sign, but if
there had been one it had been removed either
intentionally or by the storms.

Gage parked the van in a grassy area near
the door at the side of the building. There weren't
any windows near the door, so I couldn't even try
to peek inside. Something told me that even if
there would have been windows, I wouldn't have
been able to look into them. They'd probably be
blocked or painted over so someone wandering by
couldn't see inside.

"Come on," Wendy said before she hopped
out of the van. She closed her door and slid open
the van's side door next to me. "Ready?"

I tried to move, but the second I did the pain
intensified. The medicine had completely worn off.
I'd barely moved my body since the attack and it
was refusing to work.

"Travis, Gage, help her out please," Wendy said wearing a concerned look as she stared at my legs. "Maybe we need to get a stretcher?"

"No, I can do it. My body is just stiff," I said grinding my teeth together so hard it felt as though I was lightly sanding them down. I wanted to be on my own two feet instead of laying on my back when entering the building.

The building was large enough that I wasn't sure once I was inside if I'd be able to remember the way back out. I wanted to do everything I could to try to memorize how to get out of the building so if I managed to get a chance to escape, I could.

"Are you sure?" Wendy said raising an eyebrow.

"Yes, I'm sure," I said trying to sound confident. Gage stretched out his arm and helped me as I stepped out of the van. He carefully lowered me to the ground, which was only a few inches down, but it felt as though I was falling much further.

He wrapped his arm around my back and Travis went around to my other side. My feet felt as though they had pins and needles stabbing at them even though Travis and Gage were holding most of my weight.

They helped me forward. Their height difference made it awkward, but I appreciated the help. Wendy slammed the van door shut behind us and I jumped at the noise.

"Gaahhhh," I groaned as pain seared through my veins.

"Are you OK?" Gage said as he stopped and looked at me. "We can get the stretcher, it's not a big deal. I swear."

"No, no I'm OK. I'm ready."

We moved forward with Gage doing most of the work. He watched my facial expressions carefully to make sure he wasn't pushing me to do more than I could handle. The more I moved my body the more I seemed to remember how everything was supposed to work even though each step was torturous.

I was dizzy, bruised and every bone and muscle in my body ached, but I could force myself to move. We moved slowly and carefully, but I was ecstatic to be on my feet.

Wendy walked ahead and knocked on the back door. It was a strange knock, and I was sure it was some kind of secret code. She kept her eyes focused on me while we waited.

After a few seconds, the door opened and someone peeked out cautiously. Wendy blocked my view, and the person on the other side of the door said something I couldn't understand. It sounded as though it could have been another language.

Wendy said something back, and the door opened wider allowing us access. I looked out at the yard behind me. If I could have, I would have at least attempted to run away. I let out a soft sigh and turned back towards the door.

"We have one… she's hurt. Seems kind of bad. Let him know," Wendy said in a hushed voice that I could barely hear.

Wendy held the door open as Travis and Gage helped me inside the building. Travis dropped back when all three of us couldn't fit through the doorway. I gripped the doorframe lightly and pulled myself up a step while Gage gave me a little boost.

Wendy watched carefully as we walked past her and into the hallway. Once Travis was inside she closed the door and checked to make sure it was locked.

I looked down the long, dark hall that was littered with a random scattering of small lanterns. There were so few of them that they provided very little illumination, just barely enough to see our way.

I hated standing there in the near-darkness with people I didn't know. And I was so weak that if something did happen, I wouldn't be able to even attempt to defend myself.

There were doors all the way down the hallway, all of which were closed. Wendy nodded towards the empty hall as if she knew what I was thinking, "We don't use this wing for anything. It's empty."

"Oh?" I said trying to ignore the pain in my legs. They were threatening to give out. I needed to sit down before I fell down. "How come you don't use it?"

"Don't need to. At least not yet," she said turning towards me again. "Sure you don't want a stretcher? Or maybe you'd prefer a wheelchair?"

"I'm sure," I said with a tight-lipped smile. I wasn't sure why I was being so stubborn, considering I couldn't run even if I wanted to. My body wouldn't allow it. My vision still wasn't back to normal and my mind was foggy. What happened over the last several hours were beginning to fade away. Even if I would have had the path to Penn in my mind, it would have vanished. "Is the doctor close?"

Travis met my eyes and frowned, "He's on the other side of the building. Sorry."

"Of course he is." I took a deep breath and the sharp pain in my side stabbed at me. "On second thought, I will take you up on that wheelchair."

"Sure, wait here," Gage said dragging his thumb down his chin before his eyes lit up and he started to jog down the hallway.

"No problem. I'll be right here… what choice do I have?" I said trying to sound playful, but based on the look Wendy had on her face, it probably had come off as something else.

It seemed strange that Gage had to think about where to find a wheelchair, but maybe they hadn't come across many people that needed one. For all I knew, I was the first person to request it. Or perhaps they used them so much he wasn't sure where one might be at any given time.

Wendy leaned back against the wall and stared at me. She didn't even bother to try to hide it. It looked as though she wanted to ask me something, but she didn't. She just stood there watching me, and it didn't help make my legs feel any stronger.

After a few minutes, Gage rounded a corner

and pushed a squeaky wheelchair down the hall towards us. He wore a smile, but it looked creepy in the dim glowing light from the little lanterns.

I swallowed hard when he stopped abruptly in front of me. The flames glowed and danced in his eyes. He tilted his head to the side and cleared his throat, "Hop on… let's go see the Doc."

Chapter six.

Gage rolled me down the hallway as if we were in some kind of race. He moved so fast that when he made a sharp right turn, two of the wheels lifted off of the ground.

At the end of the long dark hall was a small area with a set of broken elevators. The word 'Lobby' still remained over one of the openings that would take us down another hallway. There was a little faded arrow next to it that pointed straight ahead.

I turned my head side to side as quickly as I could, attempting to memorize the route. But I was failing miserably. My brain was too foggy from having been beaten nearly to death in the woods.

We turned down a small hallway off to the side. Gage stopped the wheelchair.

"Here we are," Gage said, turning me to face a set of double doors. Wendy pushed one of the doors open while Travis pushed the other. They stepped in, allowing Gage the space to roll me inside.

It was a large room that was filled with all sorts of gadgets and things which likely didn't even work anymore without electricity. The doctor was sitting in a chair with his back towards the door. His head was down looking at something on the desk.

"This is Ros," Gage said and the doctor popped up out of his chair. He flounced over towards me like a Muppet and stopped in front of the wheelchair.

He bent himself in half so our faces were at the same level. The doctor was too close, far too close. I bit my cheek and looked towards Gage and then Wendy as though I wasn't sure if this was really happening.

His face was only inches from mine. I'm not sure I could have been any more uncomfortable than I was in that moment. I gripped the ratty arms of the wheelchair readying myself in case I had to try to wheel myself away.

"Ros, huh?" he said staring at me. "Hmm… yes. Get her on the bed. Can you tell me what happened to you, Ros?"

"Umm…." I couldn't think of a single reason why I shouldn't tell him what had happened. Wendy, Gage and Travis already knew. There would be no point in trying to purposefully hide any of it. I took a deep breath and retold as much of it as I could remember while Gage and Travis helped me onto the bed.

"He just grabbed you?"

"Yeah, he came out of nowhere, grabbed me and dragged me out into the woods. I don't remember everything that happened, much before that is a blur, but something made him mad and he started hitting me," I said seeing parts of it playing in my head as though it had been a movie.

"Do you remember anything about what he looked like? Anything of note? Maybe some kind

61

of unusual feature or a tattoo?" the doctor asked.

"We found her pretty far away from here," Wendy interrupted.

The doctor shot her a look and then tilted his head to the side. He scrunched up his face as though he suddenly smelled something terrible, "You three are free to go. She's going to be here awhile. Send in the nurse." He pointed awkwardly at Gage and then the door.

Gage nodded and then dashed out of the room. Wendy looked at the doctor to see if he was serious. When he crossed his arms, she blinked several times and then left in a huff.

I wasn't sure how I felt about any of them, but I would have preferred not to have been left alone with the doctor. The man looked like he was dressed for Halloween in his mad scientist costume. He made me nervous. When the door closed, and I was all alone with him, I shivered.

The doctor walked over and stood at the side of the bed. He looked down at me over the tops of his thin, wire-rimmed glasses.

"I'm going to examine you now, just to make sure nothing serious is going on, at least as far as I can tell," he said as he whipped out a pair of blue gloves from his pocket. When he struggled to pull them over his hands, I figured they had been reused multiple times. The gloves were just another part of his costume. He lightly touched at one of the cuts on my forehead and I winced, "Where does it hurt the most?"

"Are you a real doctor?" I said twisting my fingers against one another. The way he looked at me, I knew my words had come out wrong, "What I mean is, before all this happened what kind of doctor were you?"

"I was a pediatrician," he said with a soft smile as he dragged his palms down my arms. The look on his face made me assume he was thinking back to the life he had before the storms. He pushed on my forearm a bit, "Does this hurt?"

I shook my head just as a short woman walked in. She moved around the room fast, as if she knew exactly what she was supposed to do without being told.

"I hurt everywhere, but my side is the worst," I said pointing towards the side of my abdomen. "Everything else just feels badly bruised."

"Hmm," he said as he carefully pressed at my ribs one at a time watching my face. "Take a deep breath."

I tried to suck in air, but I stopped when the pain increased. "Mmm owww," I moaned as he delicately pressed at my side and glided his fingers up and down my ribcage.

"Well, I think you have a broken rib. Without X-rays, I can't know for sure, but, alas, we cannot do any kind of imaging. So, all I can do is offer you my best guess at a diagnosis."

"So what should I do about it?" I said trying to sit up. When the pain intensified, I closed my eyes and lowered myself back down. If I couldn't sit up, how was I going to leave this place?

"Mm-hmm… well, there isn't anything you can do about it."

"Huh?" I looked at him in disbelief. There had to be something he could do to help me.

"You'll just have to let it heal on its own. I'll give you pain meds and you can rest in one of our rooms in the south wing. There are others like you there." He walked over to the table and wrote something down on a piece of paper. "The nurse will clean and bandage your wounds. When she's finished, Wendy will be back to wheel you to your room."

I sighed, "Really? That's it? You can't like put me in a cast?"

He just laughed and waved his hand at me as if I'd told a joke. "You'll be back on your feet in no time."

"Yeah? How long is all of this going to take?" I asked worried about how soon I could get back to Penn and Carter. If I could even find my way back to them. It wasn't like I could just stay here forever.

Penn and Carter would have figured out I was gone by now. They'd be looking for me. Penn wouldn't stop looking for me.

Would he stay at the house? We agreed that if anything happened that was where we'd fight to get back to. So, if he went looking for me, I didn't think he'd go far. At least I hoped he wouldn't. I had to try to get back to our house. The sooner I could get out of here and find my way back, the better.

"A few weeks. You'll have to limit your movements so you don't aggravate it and we'll do what we can to control the pain in the meantime."

"A few weeks? I don't have a few weeks to lie around!" I said trying to get up but not making it more than an inch forward.

He cocked his head to the side, "Have somewhere you need to be?"

"Well... I don't know." I didn't know what to say. I did have somewhere I wanted to be, but I couldn't tell him about Penn and Carter. "There are just some things I need to take care of. I can't be stuck in here for weeks and weeks is all."

"Such a busy girl, with seemingly so little left out there," he said softly as though he didn't believe me.

I shook my head and searched for words to explain. But I couldn't find them.

"Hmm, well, I'm sorry but there isn't much else you can do. You'll just have to wait it out. Unless you want to leave and wander around in pain until you collapse somewhere out there. Odds are Wendy won't find you again." He tapped his chin as if he was trying to think of all my options.

"But I just—"

"Or you could stay here and let us help you get better. Then you can leave and get back to all of those things you need to attend to. The choice is yours of course, but I doubt you're strong enough to even make your way out of this building alone, how will you fend off another attack?" He turned to his papers and didn't really seem to care what I said.

"Well, I ah...."

He blew out a puff of air, "I didn't think so. Stay. I'll help you get back on your feet. You won't even have to struggle to find food, we'll make sure you're taken good care of."

I watched his arm move as he aggressively wrote on his papers. Why was he even bothering to keep records? What did that piece of paper say? Was it about me? I'd probably never know.

"OK," he said rolling backwards on his chair and spinning to face me. He crossed his arms, "Do you have any questions for me?"

"Probably a lot of questions," I said looking around at the walls.

"Let me rephrase that, do you have any immediate questions I'm able to answer about your care?"

"No, I guess not," I said, my tone rising at the end. I had so many questions about this place but none I'd probably have gotten satisfactory answers to anyway.

The pain in my side was starting to build. It was taking over my thoughts so much that all I could even think about was getting some rest.

The doctor had been right about one thing... if I would have left, I wouldn't have made it very far. Maybe not even off of the property.

"Sounds good. I'll see you again in a few days to check on you. Take care of yourself, Ros," he said, and he walked out of the room.

The nurse turned towards me and smiled as if the doctor leaving the room had been her cue to turn on. She took a small, careful step closer as if testing out how I'd react to her approach.

"Hi there honey," she said in a thick voice. She grabbed a tray on wheels and rolled it noisily along the ground. "I'm Nurse Darringer, and I'll be taking care of your cuts and scrapes today. How are you doing sweetheart? Are you in pain?"

She leaned down looking closely at my face. Nurse Darringer pointed and nodded as she scanned my skin for everything that would need treating.

"I've been better," I said biting my cheek.

The nurse put her hand on my shoulder and looked at me with eyes filled with concern. She turned towards the tray and put two pills in a small paper cup.

"This will help," she said as she poured water into another small paper cup from a plastic pitcher. First she handed me the little cup with pills.

I looked in the cup at them, feeling uncertain. "What are they?"

"Pain pills, honey. Go on now, take them. Down the hatch," she said waiting for me to pop them into my mouth so she could hand me the cup of water. I took a deep breath, shrugged and put the pills in my mouth. "That's a good girl," she said handing me the cup of water. "Now let me take care of the cuts, hmm? Mm-mm-mm, they don't look so bad."

Nurse Darringer dabbed at each one with a cotton swab before she put on some kind of gel. She placed small squares of gauze on top of the bigger cuts. When she moved down to my arm, and I saw the long cut, I tried to remember what had happened, but I couldn't. My mind was a complete blank.

67

"You're going to be all right, dear," she said when she noticed the look on my face. I knew I was going to be fine, but I was frustrated that I couldn't remember how I'd gotten the cut.

After Nurse Darringer finished, she took a step back and looked me up and down as though she wanted to make sure she didn't miss anything. Then she stepped closer and placed her hand lightly on my shoulder. I could feel the warmth of her through my shirt.

She moved her face directly in front of mine and looked into my eyes, "You're going to be fine, honey. Just fine. I can tell you're a fighter. How long you've been out there fighting?"

I made a strange noise that turned into a cough. If only she'd known what I'd been through. I wasn't a fighter. I wasn't even sure most of the time how I'd survived this long. I'd just been lucky... so far.

"Too long," I said forcing another cough, so I didn't have to say anything more.

"I'll send for Wendy. You take care of yourself now, you hear?" Nurse Darringer said as she wheeled her little cart out of the door with her.

When the door clicked closed, I shut my eyes and forced myself to sit up. I wrapped my arms around my middle trying to keep my body from moving too much, but every breath I took was almost enough to make me pass out.

It wasn't more than five minutes before Wendy walked in. She pushed the wheelchair closer and stood next to me.

"Ready?"

68

"I guess so," I said, and she stuck out her arm to offer support. At first I tried to ignore her help to show her I could do it on my own, but I couldn't. I was sure that if I didn't accept her help, I would have ended up faceplanting on the hard, linoleum floor.

I had to move slowly, but she got me into the chair without too much difficulty. If I kept my breaths controlled and short, I could tolerate the pain, or maybe the meds had simply kicked in.

"Alright, let's go," she said as she started to push the wheelchair. "Your room is all set and I even have some good news for you."

"Oh yeah? What's that?"

"You don't have to share it with anyone. Well, not yet anyway… it probably won't stay that way for long. It never does."

"You get a lot of people coming here?" I asked trying to look back at her to see if I could read her expression, but I couldn't twist far enough to see her face.

"More than you might think."

"Huh," I said not sure if she was telling the truth. Maybe she was only telling me what she thought might make me feel better about being trapped here. But then again, I don't think Wendy really cared how I felt about being here.

She pulled the wheelchair back into her thighs and looked down at me. I tilted my head up to look at her and she smirked at me. "Trust me, you're far from the first person to come in here all beat up like this."

She started pushing me forward before I

could even say anything. We moved quickly down the long hallway.

Wendy pushed me so fast that the air around me felt cold and I shivered. I hugged myself to try to warm myself but it didn't help.

My thoughts continued to drift back to how I was going to get out of this place. And even if I did, if I would ever be able to find Penn again.

This building was huge. I wasn't confident I'd easily be able to find my way out again if I had to.

There wasn't anything about this place that felt right, but at least they hadn't killed me.

I wasn't sure exactly how I was going to pull it off, but I needed to get out of here. Maybe I'd feel better tomorrow after some rest, and hopefully leaving would be as simple as someone showing me where the door was.

"Here we go. This is your room," Wendy said as she stepped out from behind me and pushed open the door in the middle of the quiet hallway.

I hated how I felt like crying. It made me feel weak, but I bit my lip and hoped it didn't show.

I didn't want to be here. Even though this place was huge, it didn't help me feel any less claustrophobic.

I wanted out. And I wanted out now.

Chapter seven.

There were two small lanterns placed on each side of the room. It was surprising how well they lit the room with so very little light pushing through the thin, ratty curtains.

If I had to guess based on the amount of light coming through the covered window, I would have said it was nearing the end of the day. Or maybe the sky was just covered with clouds, with the curtain closed I couldn't be sure which it was. All I knew for sure was that it was gray outside the window.

With everything I'd been through it felt as though time was missing. It was like the world was alternating between being on fast forward and being on slow motion. I never knew what time it was, and I'd lost track of how many hours I'd been gone from Penn and Carter.

There were two beds made up, and each had a tray on wheels next to it. It looked like your average hospital room, but without any of the equipment, lights, or people running this way or that taking care of urgent matters.

There was a small TV still attached to the upper right corner of the room. Too bad I knew it wouldn't work. Even if this place would have had electricity, there wouldn't have been anything on TV. Broadcasts were a thing of the past.

"Which bed would you like?" Wendy asked breaking the silence. "Window? Or door?"

"Window is fine," I said not sure if it mattered at all. Both beds looked equally uncomfortable, and I was going to feel trapped in this small space no matter which one I chose. "What am I supposed to do in here all day?"

Wendy laughed, "Do you like to read? Or draw? Write?"

I blinked, "Read."

"I'll get you some books. Let me help you into bed. Do you need to use the bathroom first?"

I looked at her not sure how to answer. I would have liked to use the bathroom, but I didn't want an audience and it must have shown on my face.

"Oh, don't worry, I'll gladly give you some privacy," she said as she started to roll me towards the bathroom. "Use these bars and if you need help just holler. I'll wait right outside the door. When you're finished just crack the door open."

"Oh, OK," I said, and she stepped out of the room closing the door behind her. I reached over and clicked the lock on the bathroom door, even though I assumed it probably didn't work.

I put my hand on the cold metal bar to hold myself up and sighed as I tried to move. My body instantly reacted, reminding me of my injuries as it sent pain surging through every nerve.

My side was by far the worst. The pain I felt from my broken rib made me feel sick. A tear stung as it rolled down my cheek. I bit my lip hoping to stop any more from falling. The last thing I wanted was for Wendy to know even one tear had fallen, and if they kept leaking out, she'd know.

I needed to get out of this place, but I didn't know how to get away. My body was so broken it didn't work even if I commanded it to.

I'd never experienced anything like this. How could I find my way back to Penn when the pain didn't even allow me to think straight? All I could think about most of the time was the pain.

How far could I make it in this condition? I probably couldn't even make it out of the building. I could barely get myself around the bathroom.

My only option was to put faith in Penn's words. He told me he wouldn't give up on me. Penn promised me that much. He said the words. At the time, I needed to hear him say them and I'm glad that I had. As long as I believed he was there waiting for me, I would do whatever it took to get back to him. Or die trying.

"Please don't give up on me Penn," I whispered into the back of my hand, holding the tears back. My jaw hurt as I clenched my teeth. I tried my hardest not to collapse on the bathroom floor as I gathered my strength and forced myself up. I carefully moved myself along the slightly wobbly bar, inching closer towards the wheelchair.

I didn't even know where I was or how far away I was from our place. They had driven the car for such a long time before they got here. It would take me even longer to get back to Penn unless I found a car. Even if I could find my way back, it would probably take days to get there.

There was a soft knock on the door that startled me. I gasped, and it felt as though my breath got stuck in my throat.

"Ros?"

It was Wendy.

"Everything OK?" she asked. I must have been in the bathroom longer than I realized, but that wasn't really surprising considering how difficult it was to get around.

"I'm fine... sorry."

"Do you need help? I could get the nurse if you'd prefer."

I yanked myself along the bar and lowered myself back down into the wheelchair. Carefully I pushed open the bathroom door making sure I didn't hit Wendy with it.

"That won't be necessary," I said looking up briefly to meet her eyes. I spun the wheels and slowly rolled back towards the bed.

"Are you going to be able to get around OK in here by yourself?" Wendy asked. I could feel her eyes focused on the back of my head. "It might be better if we find someone to stay with you for a few days."

"No! I mean, I'll be fine. This is fine," I said waving my hand at her. I wheeled myself over to the bed and pulled myself up using the rails at the side. Hopefully she couldn't hear my teeth grinding together as I forced myself to ignore the pain.

Once I was on the bed, I looked at her and smiled. I wanted her to see that I would be just fine on my own. But the look on her face showed she wasn't nearly as confident. She could see right through my fake smile.

She tilted her head to the side and walked backwards to the door. "Well if you're sure about it?"

"I'm one hundred percent sure."

"OK then. Someone will be here to bring you food... until then just rest. Doctor's orders," Wendy said as she slowly closed the door behind her. I wasn't sure if she had closed it all of the way, but after what had felt like too long I heard the door click into place.

I took in a long, slow breath. It was too weird being stuck in this strange place... in this strange room, and I didn't have a clue how I was going to get out. But I needed to get out and as soon as I possibly could.

Being in the bed made me feel awfully tired. I let my head fall back against the pillow and stared at the black TV screen. Before I knew it, I was asleep and dreaming of being back with Penn and Carter.

* * *

When I woke up it was completely dark in the room, all except for the two dimly lit lanterns. The light flickered on the walls creating moving shadows that made the room feel even more creepy than it already was.

I knew someone had been in the room at

some point because there was some prepackaged food sitting on the tray next to me and a small stack of books. There was also more pain medicine in a small paper cup next to a small bottle of water.

I tried to sit up, but the pain was working to hold me back. My hand darted out and automatically grabbed the pain pills. I tipped the cup into my mouth and swallowed hard.

I didn't wait for the pills to kick in before pulling myself upwards and forcing my legs over the side of the bed. Even though I was pretty sure it wouldn't help, I wanted to look out the window just in case I could spot some kind of clue that would reveal where I was. Something I could use to help me when I left.

I did everything I could to ignore the pain as I hobbled over to the window. My arms were wrapped around my middle as if I was holding myself together. Everything was so quiet in the building that I felt more afraid inside these walls than I would have outside of them. It was such an eerie feeling that I had to look behind me to make sure there wasn't anything in the room with me.

I hated the feeling of this building. It was old and it felt like there were eyes watching my every move. The building was probably filled with ghosts and spirits and poltergeists. Maybe my imagination was getting the better of me, or maybe it was the pain pills.

My hand automatically reached back for my gun, but it wasn't there. I wasn't all that surprised that it was gone. I tried to think back to when it was taken, but I couldn't remember. For all I knew it had been taken by the stranger who had beaten me and left me for dead.

I curled my fingers between the rough fabric of the curtains and slowly pulled the panel to the right. It was almost as if I was afraid to see what was on the other side. At first when I saw the lined shadows that didn't move, I didn't know what I was seeing, but then when I figured it out, I wanted to cry.

I took a deep breath and lowered my head. I hoped that maybe when I looked up again, they'd be gone.

"Dammit," I said through clenched teeth as I reached my hand out and placed it flat against the cold glass window. I moved my face closer to make sure what I was seeing was real.

On the outside of the window were metal bars. The kind of bars that were put there to keep people inside. Maybe this hadn't been a hospital, maybe it had been some kind of mental institution. Then again the bars could have been installed since the storms.

All I knew was that I didn't have a good feeling about this place. I was pretty sure they had no intentions of letting me leave here. But what they didn't know was that I wasn't going to give up that easily.

I made my way over to the door, but I already knew what I was going to find when I got there. My fingers loosely wrapped around the handle and pulled down. I silently tried to move the door open, but of course, it didn't budge.

I was locked inside.

Chapter eight.

I counted each day as the sun moved across the sky and day turned into night. Four days had come and gone since I arrived at this place. And I wasn't feeling much better as far as the pain was concerned.

Each day I watched them and kept track of their schedule. I studied them... when they came, who came, what they brought me, what they'd say, if they said anything at all. I paid attention to their every move in case it would somehow come in handy.

They brought me food and water twice a day. Sometimes it was Wendy and sometimes it was the nurse, but on the fourth day it was someone I'd never seen before.

She was tall, slender and moved awkwardly. I wasn't sure how old she was but she seemed very shy and frail. The girl hadn't said anything, but she smiled with her eyes focused on her feet as she set down my tray.

"Thank you," I said as she took a careful step forward and looked at the bandage on my forehead.

She nodded, but she didn't say anything. I watched her as she moved towards the window and adjusted the curtain. She tilted her head to the side slightly and I could have sworn her eyes shifted in my direction, but maybe that had just been my imagination.

"Excuse me," I said when I noticed my pain pills weren't on the tray. She turned to face me, grasping her hands in front of her belly. Her eyes raised only slightly off of the ground. "Where is my medicine?"

She shook her head side to side and quickly rushed out of the room.

"Hey! Wait! I need those pills!" I shouted after her but it was too late. She was gone. I wanted to shout again, louder, but when the door clicked into place, I knew it was pointless.

Even though the meds weren't anything too strong, they took the edge off the pain. I'd been resting for several days straight and the pain hadn't diminished. I wanted the pills.

Less than five minutes passed before Wendy barged into the room. Her hair was wet at the sides as though she'd just finished running a marathon. She looked at me as her shoulders bobbed up and down with each breath.

"What's going on?"

I looked at her with wide eyes. "Nothing?"

"She umm." Wendy glanced at the curtains and then looked around the room before settling her eyes back on me. "Did you need something?" she said squinting one of her eyes more than the other.

"I asked that girl about my pain meds. They seemed to have forgotten to bring—"

"Oh no, you're done with those."

I narrowed my eyes at her and crossed my arms over my chest, "What do you mean?"

"Doctor's cutting you off."

"What? Why?"

She curled up one side of her mouth, "We don't have tons of medicine here. We have to ration. He said it's time. You'll be fine."

"He hasn't even come to see me again! How would he have any idea if I'll be fine without them?" I said, but wished I could take back the words. If I never saw him again, I'd be fine with that. It wasn't like he had done anything helpful other than give me the pain pills.

"Sorry, but we just have to keep a careful count of all our medicines. He thinks you'll be able to tolerate the pain once you get used to it. It'll just be a little rough at first," Wendy said stepping over to the second bed and adjusting the blankets.

I wanted to tell her the doctor was stupid and making a mistake, but maybe it was for the best. There wouldn't be any pain meds on the outside… well, not readily available. Once I could manage the pain on my own, the sooner I could get myself out of here and back to Penn and Carter.

"Oh, while I'm here…," Wendy said putting her hands on her hips and looking down at me, "I should probably let you know that you'll be getting a roommate today."

I didn't want a roommate. A roommate would hold me back… slow things down. It would definitely make it harder for me to sneak away if there was another person in this room with their eyes on me. And I already wasn't sure how I was going to get out of the locked door or through the bars on the window.

80

"Oh," I said hoping my disappointment was obvious.

"Yeaaaah, sorry," she said not sounding the least bit sorry. In fact, she seemed kind of amused. "Limited space and all that. I'll bring her by later. She's in with the doctor right now."

I sighed and pulled my food closer. Before I even tasted it, I knew the bowl of soup was cold. But I needed to eat. Food, water and rest would help me heal faster.

I kept my eyes on Wendy as I slurped the chicken noodle soup. She raised her eyebrow as if she was waiting for a report on the quality of the food, but I just stared at her waiting for her to get so uncomfortable she'd be forced to leave my room.

"Well, I'll see you later... enjoy," she said glancing down at the bowl and turning on her heel.

"Wait," I said, and she stopped without turning around.

"Yes?"

"Oh, it's nothing really, I was just curious... where am I exactly? Like what is this place again?" I said scraping the bottom of the spoon against the bowl.

I could tell by the movements in her shoulders that she had swallowed hard, "This is like a hospital. We help people."

"I see but... why?"

"Oh, that's easy," she said turning to face me, "it's just what we do. Someone had to do it or everyone would die. The doctor just started this place to help others. We are doing what needs to be done," she said forcing a smile.

"Uh-huh. What does he get out of doing all this though? Where do the supplies come from? And the staff, why do they help?"

Wendy shrugged, "Not sure. I guess to feel like they are a part of fixing everything. To make everything right again. I'm just happy I get to help people instead of struggling out there."

I could tell she had become extremely uncomfortable with my questions. Hadn't other people asked any of these questions before? Maybe others had struggled so much out there that this seemed like some kind of oasis to them, but to me it wasn't. My oasis was back with Penn and Carter.

"Right. And where is this building located again?"

"This is Michigan. Not that any of that matters anymore. Is there anything I can get for you before I leave? I really need to get back to my work," she said stepping towards the door. She was clearly putting an end to the questions.

I knew we had driven all night to get here, but I didn't know how fast the car had been moving. It was possible we were still in Michigan, I'm not sure why she would lie about that. And even though Michigan was big, I felt better knowing I was probably in the same state as Penn.

When the door quietly clicked shut, I rolled my eyes. It was as though they were trying to hide the fact that they were keeping me here against my will. They locked the door and barred the windows, there was no way they'd be able to deny it. I wasn't fooled, and I hoped they knew that.

After I finished eating, I picked up a book from the small collection Wendy had brought me. But I couldn't read it. I couldn't concentrate. All I could do was stare at the words and try to figure out my escape plan.

Then I started wondering about my roommate. What would she be like? Would she care that she was locked in here? Having someone in the room with me was going to make it harder to find a way out of here. The last thing I needed was to share a room, but then again, for now I was trapped either way. Maybe a little company wouldn't be the end of the world.

My body jolted when I heard the doorknob being turned. As the door was pushed open I tried to shift myself up against the back of the reclined mattress so I was in more of a seated position. I wanted a good look at the person who was about to be my roommate.

Wendy was saying something so quietly I couldn't make out her words. When she stepped into view, she smiled at me as though we were the best of friends.

"Ah! You're up. I was just telling her that you might be resting," Wendy said gesturing towards the girl at her side.

The girl I assumed to be my roommate looked as though she was about my age, maybe a little older. I watched her as she looked around the room. Her eyes moved from the window, to the door, and then the bed before she settled her eyes on me.

She was tall with eyes that looked as though they belonged to a cat. Her light golden hair was pulled back into a tight ponytail. It was odd to me how clean her hair looked. When she smiled, her lips stretched beautifully from ear to ear.

"This is Nora," Wendy said putting her hand on the girl's shoulder. Then she nodded at me, "And that's Ros. You'll be great roommates, I can tell already."

My new roommate, Nora, folded her hands in front of her slim body and her smile faded. She nodded at me when Wendy gestured at the empty bed.

Nora took small, baby steps towards the bed and lightly rested her bottom on top of the mattress. It didn't appear as though she was actually putting any weight on the bed and instead was just slightly hovering over it.

The look on her face was probably similar to the one I wore when I first arrived here. She looked frightened, confused… or at the very least, not exactly thrilled to be here.

At least we had that in common.

"There are books there you can read, the bathroom is back here, and yeah, that's really all there is… for now," Wendy said refusing to look at me even though I was sure she could feel my eyes on her. Maybe she was afraid I'd start asking more questions in front of the new girl.

"How long will I have to be in here?" Nora asked.

"Until you're well again," Wendy said, and I shifted my eyes to Nora. There wasn't a single

84

thing that looked unwell about her.

Wendy took a step backwards, "If either of you need anything just let me—"

"Could you bring more books? And could you also tell me when I can get out of this room?" I said glancing at Nora.

"Sure more books, you got it," Wendy said and forced a tight-lipped smile in my direction. "Oh, and someone will come for you soon. You're probably both ready to start attending service. That should really help."

Before I could ask what she was talking about, she practically vanished from the room. Every time she spoke it just made me want to get out of here more. I needed to get out as soon as possible. How much of this could I take?

I didn't know what this service Wendy mentioned was, but I didn't think I was going to like it. And there probably wasn't anything I could do about it either. I would find out more about the service whether I liked it or not.

Once the door clicked into place, I leaned back and let my body relax. I looked over at Nora who was still lightly perched on top of the mattress.

She rubbed her fingers together and smiled at me again, "Have you been here long?"

"Four days. Tomorrow will be number five," I said, and waited for her to be surprised, but it didn't happen. She didn't seem to think it was strange I had been lying in bed for nearly five days. I wondered if maybe they had told her what had happened to me.

"Why are you here?" she asked, which

made me realize they hadn't told her anything about her new roommate. She looked at me as though she wasn't sure if she even wanted to hear the answer.

"They found me... I'd been beaten. I guess they probably saved my life," I said as I adjusted my pillow. "What are you doing here?"

"They told me they found me passed out along the side of the road. I don't remember that, I just remember waking up here with the doctor staring at me."

"Passed out?"

"It had been some time since I'd eaten... that happens to me every so often. I'd always think to myself that one time I wouldn't wake up, but thankfully that hasn't happened yet," she said with a small, uncomfortable laugh. It was like she wanted to find some kind of humor in her situation, but there really wasn't any there.

Nora stood up and looked through the pile of books. She picked one up and showed it to me. It seemed as though she was asking permission, so I nodded and she took it back to her bed.

She pressed her hands down on the bed as though she was checking to make sure it would be strong enough to hold her. The girl was so frail she could have slept on a cloud and it would have held her up.

"So what do we do here?" she asked as she turned around and scooted herself onto the bed.

"Nothing. Read, I guess," I said turning my attention back to my own book.

"Oh," she said and hugged her knees to her

86

chest. I couldn't decide if she seemed scared or not, if anything she almost seemed to be in shock. Or maybe it was just confusion. Nora was hard to read.

I put my book down on my leg and turned towards her, "Do you know anything about this place?"

She blinked several times and looked at me as though I was dumb, "No… I just got here, remember? I was hoping you could tell me what's up with this place."

I chuckled, but stopped and grabbed my side when the movements were too much. Nora watched me closely as the pain washed over me.

"Oooh, ugh," I moaned.

"Are you hurt bad?" she asked looking at my empty tray.

"Broken rib… I'll live, at least that's what they tell me. Sometimes I don't necessarily believe it though," I said and picked my book back up. It seemed the girl didn't know anything more about this place than I did. We were both stuck here, and maybe she was OK with that.

She laid back on the bed and opened her book. "Maybe we'll find out more at this service, whatever it is."

"Yeah, maybe," I said unable to stop myself from looking at the window. When would I tell her about the bars? When would I tell her that they kept the door locked?

She'd probably find out soon enough. Hopefully, she was right, and we'd learn more about this place at the service. At the very least, assuming we leave our room, I could try to discover a route out of this place.

Nora and I didn't talk much more that night, we both fell asleep reading. I didn't wake up again until I heard the door slam against the back wall as it was aggressively pushed open.

My body jolted up, and I reached for my gun that wasn't there.

Chapter nine.

Nora looked at me as though she thought for sure I had to know what was going on, but I didn't have a clue either. I tried to get myself out of my bed, but the pain and stiffness was always worse when I first woke up.

She jumped out of bed and offered me her arm. Her fingers were shaking, and I didn't know if it was because she was so thin it made her cold, or if it was because she was frightened.

"Let me help you," she said quickly, and I grabbed onto her arm.

"Please slowly exit the room," a deep voice bellowed from the hallway. I looked at Nora with wide eyes, but she just shrugged.

I'd been in this place for five days and never once had I heard these men come through the hallway. They were so loud I didn't think it was something I could have missed.

"Do they do this every day?" Nora asked quietly as she helped me off of the bed. "Wheelchair?"

I nodded. I didn't think it was even an option not to take it. "This is the first time I've heard them come by."

"Let's go ladies," the voice shouted again.

I couldn't help but grimace as she helped me into the wheelchair. She looked at me and when she was satisfied with what she saw, she stepped behind, slowly wheeling my chair towards the door.

Standing out in the hall facing me and Nora was a man dressed in all black holding what I was pretty sure was an assault rifle. He looked down at me for a second and then over my head at Nora.

"Line up, girls," he said and tilted his head to the side to indicate the back of the line.

There were two more men with guns at the front of the line and two at the back. The guns were making me nervous, especially when I didn't have my own. Although mine was nothing compared to the fire power these men were carrying.

The air felt like it was leaving the room and I was finding it hard to breathe. Even though I was out of my small room, I didn't feel any better. I still felt claustrophobic.

Lined up against the wall, standing in a perfectly straight line, were four other girls. I glanced at them, but they each seemed to be wearing a glazed over expression. As Nora rolled me to the back of the line, one of the girls looked down at me, and then at the wheelchair, before turning her eyes back to focus on mine.

"Are you royalty? Some kind of princess or something?" she mumbled, but before I could say anything the armed guy who had let us out of the room cleared his throat. He wasn't going to let anything get out of hand.

"Head out," he shouted to the front of the line and the two armed men at the front motioned for the first girl to lead the way. One armed guard walked off to one side and the second guy on the other side. They both held their guns at a specific angle as though they'd be ready to use them at a moment's notice.

Nora rolled me down the hall and even though I couldn't see them, I could hear the two guards walking right behind us. Their heavy boots slapped loudly against the linoleum floor.

The girl in front of me hopped to the side when Nora accidentally rolled me into the back of her leg. The girl spun around and glared at me, "Dammit! Watch what you're doing!"

One of the guards behind us popped forward and pointed his gun at us. He shifted the end of the barrel between Nora, the girl and me.

I opened my mouth but Nora beat me to it, "Sorry, I've never driven one of these things before."

The girl placed her hands on her hips and if she was looking for any excuse to pick a fight. Before she could take it any further, the guard pointed his gun in her direction and stared at her.

She looked him up and down, but then swallowed and stepped back into line. There must have been something she saw that made her change her mind about picking a fight. Maybe she was worried about those guns.

We all walked into a room that looked as though it had once been a church. There were pews with worn out padding on the seats, but everything else had been ripped out of the room.

There were holes in the walls where things

had once been hung. The room itself even seemed to smell of incense as though frankincense scented smoke had soaked into the walls.

The men had everyone sit in the pews except for me. They instructed Nora to roll my wheelchair up to the end of the last pew. She glanced at me and then sat down to my left.

"What is this?" I whispered but of course no one answered.

It didn't take long before a man stepped out from a door at the side of the room and stood up on top of the little stage in the front. He folded his hands in front of his chest as though he were praying, but he wore a big, forced smile on his youthful face.

The man had rounded cheeks that made him seem younger than he probably was. He looked healthy. As though he hadn't struggled even for a single day after the storms came.

I wasn't sure if the other girls could sense it or not, but there was something about this guy that was... off. Before he even said anything he already had rubbed me the wrong way.

Even though he was smiling, I felt very uncomfortable being in the same room. It felt like how I'd imagine it to be sitting in a room with someone you knew had gotten away with murder. Someone who was guilty of some horrendous crime, but managed to get off on some technicality.

When his eyes landed on me it felt as though there were hundreds of spiders crawling up and down my arms. I didn't trust him. But then again, I didn't trust anyone.

"Welcome," he said raising his hands out to the sides with his palms facing outward. "Most of us have met, but for the new faces in the room let me introduce myself, I'm Father Erik."

The girl Nora had accidentally driven my wheelchair into looked at us. It looked as though she was annoyed by our presence. She didn't want the new faces getting in the way of her special service time with Father Erik.

Everyone was so quiet I could hear my own heartbeat and I wondered if everyone else in the room could hear it too. If Father Erik noticed any of it, he pretended not to. The big smile on his face didn't waver as he looked around the room.

Nora was pressing her fingers together so hard. When she bent them backwards I couldn't believe that it wasn't causing her pain. I looked up at her, watching her jaw move up and down as she gnawed on the inside of her own cheek.

All of this was just as new to her as it was to me. And it seemed as though she didn't care for it either.

"So, so many new and beautiful faces. I can't wait to get to know each one of you. I'm sure you are wondering exactly why you are here and what it is we do here," he said speaking slowly. He paused and set his eyes on mine. "But, before we get into all of that, I'd really like to tell you how happy we are to have you all here. Some of you may have discovered this place on your own, and others may have been found or helped by our lovely team of rescuers. Let me just tell you the most important thing to know about our facility is that you, yes you, are safe here. This is the safest place on the entire planet, and you are in it. Nothing at all can hurt you as long as you are inside these four walls."

Bullshit.

Apparently, this clown didn't remember the hail and tornadoes that blew away entire cities. It wasn't like that couldn't happen again. HOME could probably cause the same sort of destruction whenever they wanted to.

It didn't matter where I was, I knew I wasn't safe. The only place that was safe for me was back with Penn and Carter.

This place could have had a twenty-foot wall constructed around it with hundreds of armed guards and I still wouldn't have felt safe. My place, was with Penn... not here.

"During your stay here, regardless of how long it is, you'll be taken care of. You will be kept safe from the outside world and all of the evildoers that still reside out there," he started to slowly pace across the small wooden stage at the front of the room. The pauses between his sentences were like torture. Even his voice scratched at my brain. "And when all is said and done, we hope that you choose to stay here with us and live in peace and harmony until the end of your days."

He looked at each one of us, and it felt like he kept his eyes on me the longest. Maybe he could see the distrust in my eyes. Maybe he could see that the second I had an opportunity I was going to leave, no matter what he said.

"My job here at the facility is to bring

everyone together. There are only so many of us left in this new world, and we must come together as one. It is our duty," he said tapping his finger into the palm of his hand, "to make everything perfect again. And the only way to do that is to do it together."

The way he spoke to us made me think he was trying to be some kind of motivational speaker. It was clear that he was attempting to make us all feel as though we were a team.

Father Erik spoke for more than an hour, and most of it sounded like the same things, just repeated in different ways. Every time it sounded as though he was winding down, he started back up again.

I was tired, and the longer I sat there the worse my pain got. It was hard to focus on what he was saying, even though I doubted much of it was anything I hadn't heard him say already. Some of his words dropped into my brain, but it was hard to pay attention.

Father Erik told us about the beliefs of the facility and how important having service every day was to bringing everyone together. He talked about how they wanted to rebuild everything and that they were making significant progress. Before we knew it, there would be a community with houses and stores and jobs.

"You're all here because we need your help. You were alone… fighting… struggling, but we are here to help. We can make all that go away. With us, you will be happy and at peace. Doesn't that sound great? Isn't that something we all want?" he said pointing and nodding as he wore a big smile.

I couldn't help but think how it felt like he was trying to trick us into believing what he said was true. That this place was just so great that we wouldn't even want to leave.

It was how I imagined brainwashing would be. The way he spoke his words and even the tone he used... everything about it just didn't feel right.

"You will all learn much more during your stay, but for now I must send you on your way," Father Erik said as he motioned towards the guards. Apparently, he was a very busy guy. I was happy to be excused even though it meant I'd have to go back to my room. "Have a wonderful lunch, and I will see you all again very soon."

He didn't ask if we had any questions, but I was tempted to ask why there were bars on the windows. Or why they felt the need to lock us in our rooms. If this place was so wonderful, they wouldn't need bars and locks, people would just choose to stay in their peaceful, beautiful place of perfect serenity.

Father Erik quickly disappeared from the room using the same side door he had entered from. Within seconds there was an armed man standing at each corner of the room, ready to get us into line and lead us back to our rooms.

My pain was so overwhelming that I just wanted to get back to my bed to rest. I didn't even care where I was, at the moment I just needed to lay down. Not to mention I was even more motivated to heal up and get the hell out of this place.

As we moved down the hallway, we went past a room that caught my attention. I hadn't noticed it the first time through the hall, but it seemed really out of place.

I narrowed my eyes and peered inside the room while Nora wheeled me by. Inside were rows of baby cribs and rocking chairs... it looked like a big nursery. The kind you might see in a hospital in a maternity ward.

There were three women in the room, that I could see, all of them moving about as though they had a purpose. I twisted my head to try to see more, but someone quickly closed the door.

I glanced up at Nora to check her expression. Nothing. Her eyes were focused straight ahead, she must not have noticed the strange room.

Why would they need a nursery? What kind of place was this? My stomach felt sick, and I trusted it enough at this point to know I needed to get out of here. And fast.

Chapter ten.

Back inside our room, Nora helped me out of the wheelchair and stood next to me as I climbed onto the bed. Once I was situated, I waved at her like she was a pesky mosquito, but she didn't move.

"What was all that," she said as she folded her arms in front of her chest.

"You're asking me? As if I should know?" I said staring at her with wide eyes. "I'm almost as new to this place as you are. I have no idea what's going on in here."

One of the last things Father Erik had told us before we had left was that we should take time to meditate and reflect on his words. But all I wanted to think about was planning my escape.

Nora shook her head, "I don't know what it is, but I have a weird feeling about this place." She hugged herself and looked at me, "Do you feel it too?"

"Yeah, I definitely feel it too," I said looking at her and shaking my head. "I'm not fooled by any of this nonsense."

Nora nodded, "I've seen things… This is going to sound absolutely crazy, but do you think they could be trying to brainwash us?"

I didn't know what to say. We were definitely on the same page but I didn't know if she could be trusted. I looked her up and down as if I might see something that would allow me to trust her, but I couldn't find anything, at least not yet. There was no flashing sign telling me that she was one of the good guys. If there were even any good guys left.

When I first met her, I wasn't sure what I thought of her, but now it seemed like we might get along just fine. Maybe we could be allies. She said exactly what I had been thinking. It was almost as if she had read my mind.

If I could convince her to leave maybe she and I could work together. Maybe we'd actually have a chance to get out of this place.

"Have you heard of a place called HOME?" she whispered as she leaned closer to me.

It felt as though a cold claw with sharp fingernails grabbed my lungs and held them tight. I was finding it hard to take in air. Her words had stunned me. I didn't know how I should respond.

Nora was a complete mystery and I wasn't sure how much I should reveal about what I did or didn't know about HOME. Even though she said she didn't like it here, that wasn't enough to rattle off every detail about myself or my past. At least not yet.

My head moved side to side before I could give it too much thought. It was as though my body was responding for me.

"Oh… HOME is this organization or whatever, that takes people in. They are working to rebuild the world under their rule. I've been there," she said rubbing her palms against her knees and looking around the room as though she was afraid they could hear her.

"Why did you leave?"

Nora shrugged, "I guess I just didn't like it there."

"And they just let you walk away?"

"Yeah."

"Huh."

She tilted her head and looked me through narrowed eyes. Perhaps she thought I'd had a strange reaction to a place I claimed to know nothing about. But I knew all too well that HOME didn't just let people leave.

"Why wouldn't they?" she asked.

I stared at her with my mouth hanging wide open, waiting for the right words to surface. For some reason, I was uncomfortable talking about HOME with someone who was practically a stranger.

Could Nora tell that I had lied? Maybe she could tell that I knew more about HOME than I had admitted to.

"I don't know… maybe they would, I don't know anything about it. I just don't get the same feeling from this place," I said turning to look at my feet so I didn't have to look at her. I rubbed at my sore rib, trying to distract myself from the conversation I didn't really want to be having.

"Yeah, I don't know. The doctor told me I could leave if I wanted, but that I should stay for a while. He said I should get well first, and then I could decide. He also told me I'd probably end up loving it here," she said, her voice soft.

I looked into her eyes, "And what do you

think of it so far?"

Nora shrugged and looked towards the window.

"Do you want to leave this place?"

"Don't you?"

"Yes," I admitted.

Nora coughed lightly and looked towards the door as if she expected someone to barge in. Then she turned back to me, "Do you know anyone on the outside? Like somewhere we can go?"

"Um… no, not really," I lied. She stared at me and it almost seemed as though she didn't believe me. "Do you?"

"No."

The doorknob jiggled and fear instantly surged through my veins. It felt as though I had been caught doing something wrong and I was about to get into trouble. Had they somehow been listening in?

I sat up and tightened my fists. My body didn't relax when I heard the wheels of the food cart squeaking as it was rolled inside our room. When I saw the woman who didn't speak enter the room, I kept my eyes focused solely on her.

She didn't say anything as she put packaged foods down on my tray and then the same things on Nora's tray. I watched her as she slowly pushed the squeaky cart out of the room. It was the first time I noticed the gun resting against the back of her hip. It glimmered at me as though it was winking at me. The quiet woman was armed.

All sorts of ideas of how I could get that gun started flooding through my mind. If I could get my hands on that gun I could have a real shot at escaping this place.

I took a deep breath and turned my head so I could look at Nora, "I need some kind of plan."

She bit her fingernail keeping her eyes downward. It looked as though she was considering her options. Nora closed her eyes for a long moment before she glanced towards the door and then at me.

"But where would we go? What would we do? I'm not sure how far we'd get just the two of us."

"I have a few ideas."

"Oh?" she said with a sly smile.

I didn't want to tell her anything more. At least not yet. She didn't need to know Penn was out there waiting for me… hopefully.

I watched her carefully, "I know a place. Somewhere we can go for help. You in or not?"

She smiled and grabbed a package off her tray. Nora put the foil packaging to her teeth and ripped it open, "Oh yeah," she smiled, "I'm in."

Chapter eleven.

After we finished eating, Nora paced for at least twenty minutes before she came and sat at the foot of my bed. She looked at me and then her eyes shifted down to my side.

"How's the pain?"

I frowned, "It's been worse. We need a plan."

"Window?" Nora asked, and I shook my head. She didn't know yet.

"Look," I said as I flopped my hand towards the curtains.

Nora stood up and walked to the window. She turned around and looked at the door before she slowly peeled the curtains apart.

"Oh… oh crap. This is worse than I thought," she said and quickly let go of the fabric. "Yeah, OK, so that's not going to work. Then there is only one other option. The door."

I nodded. The bars on the window were definitely going to make things harder for us. I had to assume they were on most windows, if not all of them. It wasn't like we'd get the chance to look around for a window that didn't have bars on it. We didn't have that kind of freedom. Whatever our plan would be, it would have to involve leaving through the door.

I pushed my fingertips into my forehead, as

if rubbing my head hard enough might make the best plan appear. "But when... and how?" I asked hoping maybe Nora had a suggestion.

She tapped her finger lightly against her bottom lip. I could tell she didn't have any more ideas about escaping than I did.

"It's going to take time," I said interrupting her thoughts. "We need to wait. And watch."

"Yeah, we might only get one shot to do this right," she said looking as though she might be having second thoughts. She swallowed hard and forced a look of determination to spread across her face, "OK. We can do this."

"You don't have a gun, or a knife or anything, do you?" I asked, but I knew they probably had taken it from her if she had arrived with one. She shook her head. "Me either, but I saw that woman, the one that brings us food—"

"Yeah?"

"She had a gun strapped to her hip... like an old western holster type do-hickey," I said lightly tapping the hip on my good side.

Nora smiled. It looked as though she was impressed with my observation, but it wasn't like the woman had been trying to hide the fact that she was carrying a gun.

We were still a long way from getting away from this place. Even if we could disarm the woman, we still had to make our way to the exit.

When they brought me here, we had entered through a side door. Wendy, Gage and Travis led me down a long hallway before we turned to make our way to the doctor. After my visit it was another

104

long walk to get me to this room. I had tried to remember the way, but I didn't think I'd be able to if it came down to it. Especially under any kind of pressure.

"How did you get inside the building?" I asked leaning back against my pillow.

Nora frowned, "I don't remember."

"You don't remember? Like nothing at all?"

"No… I wasn't awake," she said looking away from me.

"Oh, that's right. Damn."

"Do you remember how you got in?"

I shook my head, "Not really. I came in through a back door somewhere, but I don't remember the way."

She stood up and started pacing, "Well that doesn't make things any easier for us does it? So maybe we can get the gun, but we still have no idea which way to go… well, this is going to go well."

I let out a small laugh, but I stopped the second I could feel the pain start to pinch at my side. Everything was on hold, not only because we didn't have a plan, but because I was still limited in what I could do.

With each day that went by, I did feel a little better, but I didn't have weeks to sit around waiting until I was back to one hundred percent. I didn't need to wait… once I got back to my place with Penn and Carter, I could rest.

Now I just needed to get to a point that would allow me to move quickly enough to get out of whatever this place was. It was going to be a challenge, that much I knew. There wouldn't be bars on the windows and they wouldn't lock the doors if they didn't care if we left or not.

If this place was somehow linked to HOME, maybe I'd never get out of here. But since they hadn't killed me on sight, and instead they actually helped me, I just didn't know.

"When do you think you'll be ready?" Nora said with a quick nod towards my side.

I wanted to lie and say it was fine, and that I would be ready as soon as possible, but if I was a liability to our escape, she should be aware of that fact. "I'm not sure. It's bad, but improving. The doctor said it was broken, and that it could take weeks to fully heal. But I don't have weeks."

"He didn't have X-rays so how could he know?" she asked, and I shook my head. It seemed as though she wanted me to be ready. She wanted to go as soon as possible too. "Maybe he's wrong then. Maybe it's not broken."

"I hope you're right," I said as I lightly pushed on my rib to see how much pressure I could tolerate. It was more than I had anticipated, but maybe my adrenaline was pumping at the idea of getting out of this bizarre place. "The sooner we can get out of here, the better."

She glanced at my fingers pushing against my shirt. "We'll wait."

"We'll watch them. Learn anything and everything we can about them and their routines. We'll look for our best chance at escape. It'll take time, but I think it gives us the best odds of actually coming up with a plan that works," I said as though

I was in charge of this operation.

Nora's bed creaked as she sat down. "You're right. We can do this, but I have to admit, I'm nervous about where we'll go once we are out. I wish I knew more about what to expect once we are out of here."

"Let's not worry about that for now. We can worry about it if we ever get out of here," I said quickly. I knew exactly where I was going to go, but I didn't know what I would do about Nora just yet.

* * *

Over the next several days, Nora and I did exactly what we said we would. We waited. We watched.

We carefully, meticulously paid attention to every little detail in the routines we could. First it was breakfast, then morning service with Father Erik, followed by meditation in our room, free time and dinner. It was always the same thing.

It seemed as though the other girls that went to service with us were happy to be here. Or at least they pretended to be. Even the girl who was angry when Nora accidentally drove my wheelchair into her, smiled at us every morning.

She seemed like a different person than when I'd first met her. More at peace. Less angry. I watched her when Father Erik spoke to us... she hung on his every word. She was far more trusting

107

of the people inside this place than I would ever be.

I worried constantly that they could tell Nora and I didn't have the same dedication the other girls had. We weren't in the same zombie-like state that the other were in and they must have been able to see that.

Even when we tried to fake it, I was pretty sure they saw right through us. Whatever brainwashing techniques they were doing seemed to be working, just not on Nora and me.

Maybe it was because I wanted to get out of their facility so bad that I couldn't think or listen to what they were saying. I didn't even care to hear their words because I knew it was all lies and tricks.

The other girls in here probably didn't have anyone on the outside waiting for them like I did. If they had, they'd want to get out too.

It seemed strange to me that the only other outsiders I'd seen inside the facility were girls. Where were all the boys? Perhaps they kept them in a separate wing... but why?

Whenever Nora and I were left alone in our room, locked away until the next service, I worked on walking and building up my strength. I practiced moving across the room, ignoring any of the pain that would try to surface. If I controlled my breathing, I could manage to walk almost normally.

Moving from sitting to standing and back again on my own was difficult. The first several times I did it Nora had to spot me, but each time it became easier than the last. I learned which ways I could turn that would be more comfortable and which ways would cause me ridiculous amounts of pain.

Less than two weeks after arriving, I was able to do everything myself. I didn't even need to use the wheelchair anymore, but the only person that knew that was Nora.

She was sitting on the floor with her back to the door listening to anyone that might pass by our room. I could always tell when she heard something because she put her book down and her eyes would get wide. She'd only blink once every twenty seconds or so, as she focused on whatever it was in the hallway.

I'd stop walking to watch her but I couldn't ever read her blank expression. I had to patiently wait for her to report what she'd heard once she picked up her book. Usually it wasn't much of anything.

This time she didn't grab her book. She didn't blink and her eyes darted up towards the door handle. She launched herself off of the floor and waved at me while grabbing my wheelchair.

Nora pushed the chair towards me. I grunted when she hit me in the back of the knees and I dropped down onto the seat. My side felt better, but not enough for the rough movements. I had to hold in my howl since I didn't know what was going on.

"Sorry," she whispered as she grabbed the handles and started wheeling me towards the bed. When we heard the door open, she froze in place. We hadn't made it back to our beds.

"Good afternoon," the voice said, and I cranked my neck to see who had entered our room. Standing there looking at us with his head tilted to the side was the doctor. Nurse Darringer was standing behind him with the same tilt to her head. They both had a suspicious look on their face. "What's going on in here? Should you be out of your bed?" he asked as his feet padded slowly against the floor making his way closer to us.

"Probably not, but I had to use the bathroom," I said pointing at the bathroom door. "She was helping me back into bed when you burst in."

I could feel Nora's eyes on the back of my head.

"Not... a problem, not a problem at all," he said as he scribbled something on his notepad.

I tried to look at what he was writing but he tilted it so I couldn't see. If I would have been a little braver I would have asked, but he probably wouldn't have told me the truth anyway.

"One you're back in bed, I'd just like to check your injury and make sure everything seems to be healing as it should. How have you been feeling? I see you are getting around a little better at least."

I shrugged, "Not great... my side still hurts."

"On a scale from one to ten, ten being the worst pain you can imagine, where would you rate your pain?" he said while Nurse Darringer made her way to the other side of my bed. She pulled the blanket down and motioned for me to get into the

110

bed.

Nora offered her arm as I pulled myself out of the wheelchair. I turned around and scooted myself back on the bed making sure to groan at every opportunity. Nora glanced at me and walked away to give the doctor more room.

"I don't know like a seven, I guess? Maybe an eight," I said when I worried that a seven might not sound so bad to the doctor. The truth was it was probably more like a five, but he didn't need to know that.

He smiled, "Great... great. Love when my patients are improving. OK I'm going to just do a quick examination on your side."

I nodded, and he slowly moved his hands towards my side. My eyes shifted downward to avoid watching as he pushed around at my aching bones. I grimaced each time he pushed his fingers into my side. It almost seemed as though he was getting some kind of sick pleasure from torturing me, but hopefully I was imagining that.

His eyes shifted towards Nurse Darringer and she nodded before looking at me with concern-filled eyes. She took my hand into hers and gave me a quick, sweaty squeeze.

"Mmm hmmm, OK. Well, my official diagnosis is that you are going to live," he said with a wink and the most fake laugh I'd ever heard. The doctor looked up at Nurse Darringer and she let out a small chuckle as she waved her hand at him.

"Yeah, I think I'm going to pull through," I said but their laughing stopped as though I had been speaking in another language. I guess only the doctor could make pathetic attempts at humor.

"Now, let's see how our new girl Nora is doing," he said turning around and bending his knees, slightly lowering himself to her height. He looked at her as though he thought she was an eight-year-old girl.

Her eyes were rounded as she stared back at him. It looked as though she wanted to take a step back, but there was nowhere to go with her bed directly behind her.

"Well, your color is good. You're up on your feet, that's good too. Dizzy?"

Nora shook her head.

"Have you been eating?" he said tiling his head to the side sharply.

"Uh, of course," she said as if he thought the reason she'd passed out from not eating had been by her choice.

"Good. Have you been weighed?"

She shook her head again, "Not since I got here."

"Hmm… well, we'll have to get you back down to my office soon for a weight check. Unfortunately," he said glancing over his shoulder at Nurse Darringer who was shaking her head, "I don't have time today, but I'll send Wendy for you soon."

"Sure, OK, if that's really necessary," Nora said sounding nervous.

The doctor crossed his arms in front of his body and looked back and forth between Nora and me. "You're both doing much better than I expected. You know, you are both so lucky to be here. If it wasn't for the facility, you'd probably both be dead."

When neither of us said anything, he looked uncomfortable and laughed. Nurse Darringer joined in, and they both stared at us as their laughter sent a creepy chill up and down my spine.

I took a quick, awkward breath and chewed on my cheek. Nora turned away and climbed up onto her bed. I was pretty sure she found it all as bizarre as I had.

Their laughs stopped abruptly, and they turned towards the door as though their exit had been choreographed. "We'll see you both again soon. Take care, and be sure to let Wendy know if you need anything or if you need to see me. She'd be happy to set up an appointment. Until next time," he said with a floppy salute.

"Take care of yourselves, now," Nurse Darringer said following far too closely to the doctor. Although he didn't seem to mind.

Neither of us said anything to either of them. It was as though we had been stunned by the whole experience.

My body actually jerked when the lock clicked into place behind them. It wasn't more than two minutes after they left that there was a knock at the door.

Chapter twelve.

Nora and I looked at one another. Why would anyone bother to knock? There wasn't anything we could do to let them in since the doors were locked. All they had to do was just walk right in.

I could hear the doorknob being twisted and then the bottom of the door brushing against the tiled floor as it was pushed open. Maybe someone was bringing our food, but it wouldn't have fit the schedule.

When I saw the man dressed all in black, I blinked several times before I realized it was Father Erik. He looked different up close and in our room.

He was shorter and slimmer than I had thought. When he was up on stage his presence must have made him seem bigger than he actually was.

Father Erik looked at me with eyes that glowed like blue tinted diamonds. He tilted his head down slightly and raised the corner of his mouth.

"Hello girls," he said folding his hands in front of his stomach.

"Hi," Nora and I both said at almost the same time.

He smiled at her and then turned his head so he could show me the same fake smile. "You both

114

look like you are doing well."

I scooted myself back into a seated position as he moved closer to my bed. For some reason it felt strange reclining in his presence. He rested his hand on the rail at the foot of my bed.

Even though he was about two feet away from me, it still felt like he was too close. I hated the way he looked at me. It made me shiver and my insides tighten.

I don't know what it was, but it felt like snakes had climbed out of his pockets and were slithering across my bed. They were trying to find their way up my body and into my brain so they could discover what I was thinking.

I felt it so strongly I looked down at the sheets to make sure it was just my imagination. He smirked at me as though he could read my mind, but of course he couldn't. It was more likely I was giving away too much with my body language.

"You're probably wondering what I'm doing here." His eyes firmly locked with mine.

I nodded and I was pretty sure I saw Nora's head bobbing out of the corner of my eye. When he was this close to me, it was as though I could feel his hypnotic powers radiating from his whole body. But thankfully I was still able to keep my shield up and push it away.

Father Erik cleared his throat, "Once a week I try to make a special visit with all our new friends. I like to check in with them and make sure everything is going well, or if there is something I can help with as far as the transition from the outside world to our wonderful community is concerned. As you both know, it's not easy out there. It can come as quite a shock when you come in here and you are no longer struggling."

He paused to look at both of us in turn. It was as though he was checking to see how we felt about his words. He was letting them sink in before he chose his next sentence.

My mouth felt as though it was stuck in place. I didn't even know if I should say something.

"Our facility is like none other—"

"Are there other places like this?" Nora interrupted. I quickly twisted my head to stare at her. She knew there were others. Nora had brought up HOME to me. What was her angle? What was she trying to get out of him?

"I have been told there are others, but I have not experienced them for myself. Lucky for me, I have been blessed to be with this facility and only this facility. Why would I need to leave? Or want to leave? We have things that I'm sure other places cannot offer, such as a smooth running, friendly community. We have bountiful food, and medicines. I'd go so far as to say we are probably the only organization that has a qualified doctor."

Nora hugged herself, "I see."

"Have you experienced any of the others?" Father Erik asked looking at her.

"No," she answered instantly.

"How about you?" Father Erik said turning to look at me with his penetrating eyes.

"No," I said shaking my head. I was worried I hadn't sounded as convincing.

He smiled and started pacing, "Being with other people can be scary at first, but I assure you we all want the best for each other. It'll take time for you to trust us, and I understand that. We all want the best… I want the best for you both, too. Everyone who comes into our facility goes through that same… um… adjustment period. The one you are going through now. It takes each person a different amount of time to mesh with the others… but I've noticed one thing about the two of you."

"What's that?" I asked wrapping my arms around my middle.

He chuckled, "You both seem to be taking longer than what is typical. Is there anything either of you would like to talk about? Maybe there is something I can help you understand that will help the process along. If you don't want to talk now, we can always meet in my chambers."

Father Erik pointed at the door as though he'd whisk us away right now if we wanted to. Leaving this room with him was definitely one of the last things I'd want to do.

"No, I'm good… this place is good. I have a broken rib," I blurted out as if that would somehow be an excuse as to why I wasn't fitting in as well as he wanted me to.

I could feel Nora's eyes on me, but then she cleared her throat and the heat on the side of my head was gone. "I'm fine too… it was really rough out there, you're right. There were days I didn't eat, I hallucinated, it was terrifying. But since being in here, things are getting much better."

"That's so great to hear, I mean the part

117

about you getting better," Father Erik said with a chuckle. "I'm sure you'll both do great here once you are back to your normal selves. Like I said, everyone adjusts at a different pace, but please keep in mind that my door is always open."

He looked back and forth as though he was hoping one of us might accept. After a few moments, he tapped his knuckles on my footrest and held his hands with his palms out.

"Thanks, I'll keep that in mind," I said clasping my hands together so tightly I felt it in my forearms.

"Yeah, me too," Nora said, and his eyes shifted over to her. It was as though he'd forgotten she was even in the room.

"Good... good. I'm glad to hear that. Well, that's all I have for now, I'll see you both at the next service. Since I have a little free time I'm going to have a surprise visit with some of the other girls. It usually brightens their day to get to have an open and honest chat with me. I hope you both get to that level too," he said and I couldn't help but think that I was in some kind of cult. Perhaps once I achieved a certain rank, I would move up to something better than being locked in a room with bars on the window.

I cleared my throat, "Um, Father Erik, before you go...."

"Yes?" he said taking several small, interested steps in my direction. The pleased look on his face made my skin crawl.

"I was wondering... why are there only girls here?"

I could feel Nora's eyes on me again. This time her gaze was stronger, she was burning a hole right into the side of my head, or at least it felt that way. I knew what she was thinking. She was wondering why I hadn't kept my mouth shut, and she was probably right about it. I probably should have.

Father Erik look at me through narrowed eyes as if he didn't understand what I was asking, but then he laughed. "Oh! I see. You haven't been outside of this wing of our facility, have you?"

I shook my head.

"Right. This is the women's wing," he said as if that should explain everything. "Well now, I should really go. Have a wonderful rest of your day, girls."

He waved and quickly disappeared from the room. The way he spun around and flew out of the room made me think of Dracula flipping his cape and pivoting to exit a room or turn into a bat.

"That was awkward," Nora said softly after the lock clicked into place. I didn't know why everyone who left tried to silently move the lock. They must have known we would have tried the door by now. They just had to know that we knew we were locked inside, but if we asked, I'm sure they would have had an excuse.

"Yeah," I said, but she crossed her arms and looked at me.

"Not him, well, him too, but I meant your question."

I smiled and looked down at my hands, "Sorry, but it just seems so strange to me."

"This whole place is strange," she said and laid back against her pillow. "Even the way Father Erik talks... his voice. Ugh."

"They're trying to brainwash us. That's how he's supposed to talk," I said as if I somehow knew that to be true. In a way, it felt similar to the how everyone at HOME seemed to have been programmed to act a certain way. In fact, it was a lot like that.

Nora nodded and put her thin arm behind her head. "You're probably right, but we don't really want them to know that we know that, do we?"

"No... I guess not."

"So try to play along a little better, would you?"

I nodded.

"Before it's too late."

I tilted my head, "Too late?"

"Before they realize we aren't going to be brainwashed. That it's not going to work on us."

"That's why we need to get out of here."

There was a long pause before Nora sucked in a deep breath and sat up. She turned her body, so she was facing me.

Nora twisted her fingers against one another. Her voice was low, "I'm sick of waiting. It's time. Let's get out of here."

I looked at her, unable to stop the corners of my mouth from curling up. It struck me like a bolt of lightning.

I had an idea.

Chapter thirteen.

I knew that we would need a weapon if we wanted to get out of here. Two would be ideal, but I only knew where we might be able to get one… the woman that brought us our food.

Nora hopped off her bed and onto mine. It was awkward having her so close to me, but it didn't seem as though she felt the same. There were only a few people I ever liked having close to me and that list had been drastically reduced. It was now down to two people. Penn and Carter.

I tilted my head and looked at her with a raised brow. If she noticed my uneasiness she ignored it. I shook my head and focused on my plan.

"We need a weapon… a gun," I said even though I was stating the obvious.

"Well, problem solved," she said slapping her hands against her thighs. She rolled her eyes, "If only I would have thought of that."

"Shh," I said waving my hands as though I was batting away her pesky, sarcastic words. "The woman that brings our food… she has that gun on her hip. It's in a holster, but together, I'm fairly certain we could disarm her."

Nora looked at my side, "Even in your condition? The woman looks tough, the strong, silent type, you know?"

"We'll have to take her by surprise, I think it'll work," I said trying to sound confident. "Once we have the gun, we run out, closing the door behind us, which should lock her inside."

"Right," Nora said nodding and stretching her fingers back as though she was ready to go. "Then what?"

"That's about all I've planned so far. I don't know how to plan beyond that point, because I don't know what to do once we are in the hall. All I know is that once we have the gun, we need to navigate the halls, avoiding everyone until we can find the way out of this place. How hard can it be?" I said with a shrug.

"Are you forgetting about those armed guards?"

I shook my head, "No, but I haven't seen any except for the four that take us to service."

"We don't see much, even when we are out of this room." Nora frowned, "This place is big... it's kind of like a maze."

I knew she was right, but we had to try. We had to bet on the fact that we could make it out, either unnoticed or with the help of the gun. Hopefully unnoticed.

Whenever we went to service, the halls were mostly empty. Once in a while I'd see someone passing by, but usually it was just us and the guards.

"We take the gun, lock her in and go, just run. Anything to get out of here. I'll use the gun if I have to. Avoid the armed guards at all costs. Have we seen anyone else that has been armed?" I asked rubbing my forehead, trying to remember if I had noticed anyone else with guns.

The Doctor hadn't been, nor had Nurse Darringer. Father Erik hadn't appeared to be carrying anything either, although that didn't mean that they weren't armed, just that I hadn't seen anything.

I was pretty sure Wendy had been armed, as well as Travis and Gage. And then, again, the armed guards that brought us to service every morning. And their guns were major. Definitely more powerful than the pistol we'd get from the food lady.

"The group that brought me here was armed, and as you know, the guards... who have you seen that was armed?" I asked keeping count on my fingers.

"I'm not sure... I don't remember," she said with a small frown. I'd forgotten she said she was passed out when they brought her into the facility.

"That's OK. We want to avoid everyone, armed or not. I think we have to assume that everyone is armed."

Nora nodded and hugged her knees tightly. She looked nervous. Maybe she wanted to back out, or maybe the talk of weapons was freaking her out. And I couldn't say I blamed her... it was a risk. But I was willing to take it.

"Everything OK?" I asked.

"Yeah, of course."

"Do you want to back out?" I said each word slowly. I wanted her help. Maybe I even needed it. The two of us would have a better shot than I would going it alone, at least that's what I told myself.

It wasn't like I was going to give up. I was going to go with or without her.

"No! Of course not! I'm totally in... I just, well, don't want to get killed," she said directing her eyes down to her fingernails.

"I don't want to get shot either," I said with a small smile. "But I want to get out of here more than anything. I have to take the risk. I don't feel like I have a choice."

Nora bit the nail of her index finger nervously, but looked up at me without blinking. She looked determined. "Me too. Yeah, me too."

"Yeah? You sure?"

"I'm sure. I couldn't be more sure."

"Tomorrow then. When she comes to bring us our food. We'll be ready."

She tilted her head slightly, "What do we do?"

"I'll hide in the bathroom and once she passes me, I'll hit her over the head with something. You be ready to take the gun off of her...," I thought for a moment, "left hip."

"Then what?"

It was as though she wanted as many of the specifics as I could give her. She wanted to visualize how it would play out.

"Then we walk out the door."

"Check first to make sure the coast is clear," Nora added with a smile.

"Yes... yeah, right. We can do this," I said smiling. "Navigating this place shouldn't be all that hard. I mean, it used to be a hospital or something, right? Any of the bigger halls should lead to an exit, I would think."

Nora rubbed her palms together. She looked as though she was ready to give it a go at that very moment, and honestly I was too.

Whenever the armed guards led us to Father Erik's church-like room, we almost never saw anyone else in the halls. I assumed everyone was always locked up, except those who worked for the facility. And as long as we could avoid those people, I believed we could make it out.

"But when we are out of here, then what? Where do we go? I don't know anyone, and if you don't know anyone…" Nora said wearing a look of concern that grew with each passing second. She always came back to worrying about who was out there, but I still wasn't ready to tell her, at least not exactly.

"What are you afraid of out there?"

"I don't know… starving."

"It'll be OK. I might know someone," I said quietly, and her smile returned.

The look on her face quickly turned serious. She drummed her fingers on her shin, "I had a feeling you knew someone out there, even when you said you didn't."

I bit my lip. For a second I worried that I should have kept it to myself longer, but when the walls didn't come crashing down around me I felt as though maybe things would be fine. After all, Nora was harmless. She wanted out of here just as badly as I did.

Once we were out of this place, I'd figure out the rest. For now, all that mattered was getting us out of the facility.

I cleared my throat and looked into her eyes, "I'll take the gun… once you disarm her, give me the gun."

"Why?" she said looking as though she suddenly didn't trust me.

"Will you shoot if you have to?" I asked cocking my head to the side. Since the second I saw her, it didn't seem as though she would hurt a fly.

"Will you?" she countered widening her eyes and crossing her arms.

The words came out of my mouth without hesitation, and I almost surprised myself.

"I will."

Chapter fourteen.

It was after service and I knew it wouldn't be long before the woman with the gun would be bringing the food to our room. I was rubbing my palms on my knees to keep my hands dry.

The armed woman was the one who typically brought our lunch, so I hoped everything would go as usual. I hadn't even bothered to mention to Nora that I had some worries that something might not go according to plan. She probably had the same concerns, but wasn't telling me.

Before we left for service, Nora and I looked for things we could use to knock out the lunch lady, but everything was nailed down. The only thing we could pick up was the lanterns that lit the room, which we considered, but worried they might start a fire and set off an alarm or kill the lunch lady. We didn't want her dead, we just wanted the gun, and our freedom.

When we checked the bathroom, I saw the towel bar. It seemed like it might be our only option, if we could even get it out.

It was a little loose, but not enough to make removal easy. We pulled and pulled and it wouldn't budge. I wasn't sure if we could do it, considering my weakened state, but when it finally shifted slightly and a small part of it pulled out of the wall, we both smiled.

It had taken at least an hour and all of our weight, but we managed to get it free. The removal process had broken away part of the drywall, and it was obvious that it had been removed. I propped it back into place as best as I could just in case someone might stop by and want to look inside the bathroom. But, of course, nobody did.

Now that it was almost time for lunch, I walked into the bathroom and removed the bar. Nora was standing around the corner near our beds and out of sight. I hoped she'd be ready to grab the gun, just in case I failed at my part.

The bathroom door was open about halfway and I was hiding behind the door. It seemed as though it was taking longer than usual for the woman to bring our lunch but when the doorknob finally twisted, I wished it would have taken her longer.

My breath felt as though it was stuck in my throat as I tightened my grip around the warmed metal bar. The door slowly opened and the woman with the gun walked past the bathroom without noticing I was hiding inside.

I soundlessly stepped out of the bathroom and raised the bar above my head. She must have heard something or seen my shadow because she spun around and looked right into my eyes.

For a second I felt as though I was frozen in place. I watched her hand as it moved in slow motion towards her gun.

I swung the bar downward, aiming for the top of her head, but she stepped to the side. Her other arm automatically moved outward in an attempt to deflect the blow but I still hit her arm with everything I had. It looked as though she was about to scream out in pain but before she could open her mouth, Nora launched herself towards the woman taking her by surprise.

I dropped the bar and reached for her gun, but Nora had been faster. Our eyes met for a split second and she seemed like a totally different person than the one I'd been sharing this room with. This Nora didn't fear anything. She looked quite capable of taking care of herself.

"Hit her already!" Nora said glancing at the bar.

I shook my head. For some reason, I couldn't hit her when she was laying there looking at me with her big, scared eyes. She didn't have the gun anymore, Nora had it. It just didn't seem like there was much, if anything, she could do about it.

"Ugh!" Nora said as she stuck the gun in her waistband and grabbed the bar. She quickly raised it up in the air before the lunch lady could even move to get away, and hit her right in the middle of the head.

I stared at them both, stunned. I couldn't even believe my eyes.

When the lunch lady's eyes spun in circles, I knew it had really happened. It appeared as though she was trying to look in every direction at the same time.

It seemed impossible, but the lunch lady tried to stand up. She wobbled towards the door, trying to get away as though her life depended on it.

Nora raised the bar, but before she could strike her again, the woman's eyes rolled back and closed. She collapsed down to the floor with a thud.

I looked at Nora. If I had time for second thoughts, I would have had them, but there wasn't time. We had to get out of there.

"Let's go!" I said looking at the still open door behind us. It had taken us far longer than we had planned to disarm her, no thanks to me, but it seemed as though the ordeal had gone unnoticed.

Nora took the gun back out and held out both weapons. "Pick," she urged.

I looked at the gun and then at the bar. I don't know why I did it, but I took the bar.

Nora had acted more quickly than I had. I couldn't ignore what I had seen. I'd failed where she had succeeded. Hopefully I wasn't making a mistake.

"Have you ever used a gun before?" I whispered as we carefully made our way to the door.

"Yes, but not a lot," she said peering out from the doorway. "Coast is clear... come on," she said as she slithered out of the doorway.

I followed her, our feet barely making any sounds as we walked down the mostly dark hallway. All of the doors around us were closed, but I still couldn't help but think of the girls on the other side of each one.

It felt wrong to leave while they were all

trapped inside, but I knew if we opened the doors it would cause a panic. If there was anyone inside their room that wanted to leave they might make too much noise in their excitement. And if there were girls inside that wanted to stay they might make too much noise because they'd see us escaping. I was pretty sure they would go to extremes to try to stop us.

We had no choice but to keep going. Maybe they were all happy here anyway. Maybe they all wanted to stay. That's what I kept telling myself.

I needed to get out of here. I had to see Penn and Carter again, there wasn't a single risk I wasn't willing to take.

"This way," Nora said after peeking around one of the corners where the hallway intersected with another.

"Look!" I said pointing to a sign that must have remained from the hospital before it was converted to the facility, as they called it. On the sign was the word 'lobby' painted in red, next to an arrow that pointed to the right. I could almost feel the fresh outside air blowing against my skin.

Nora smiled and turned towards the lobby. She stopped abruptly and looked nervous. Nora paused and turned to me, "What if there are a bunch of them sitting in the lobby? Maybe that's the wrong way to go!"

"I don't know," I said shaking my head to the side. "Probably better to check it out than continue going in circles. Look how close we are!"

"We're not going in circles," she said as

though she was offended by the comment.

"Well, not yet, but who knows?" I said nudging her with my elbow.

She held up her gun and carefully moved forward, keeping her body tight to the wall. When she got to the end of the hallway, she looked around the corner.

I tightened my grip on the metal bar as though I was expecting a fight. If they came, I had to be willing to use the bar. All I had to do was think about how close to the exit I was and swing.

I was already imagining my reunion with Penn and Carter. All I had to do was get out of the facility.

"All clear," she said with a half-grin.

"Go, go, go!" I whispered feeling the urgency in every bone in my body.

She stepped out, and we ran towards the exit, trying to keep the sounds of our feet hitting the floor to a minimum, but Nora seemed just as anxious to get out as I was. We were both probably far too noisy, but we were almost there. I could see the door.

"Hey!" a girl shouted at us from behind a small desk at the back corner of the large lobby. "You aren't supposed to be out here! Who let you out?"

She started walking towards us, waving at us to come back. The look on her face quickly changed. She must have realized we were trying to escape, and I was pretty sure she had seen the gun.

Nora spun around and pulled the trigger as though she'd done it a million times. I watched as the girl pressed her hands against her forehead and her body sank to the ground.

"Go!" Nora said pushing the door open and holding it for me. When the cool air hit my face, I felt a new energy fill my veins. I was ready. And I ran faster than I ever had in my entire life.

Chapter fifteen.

I followed Nora down a small grass hill towards a patch of trees in the not-too-far distance. Even though the trees weren't all that far away, since we were in the wide open it seemed they were further away than they actually were. It was like we were running on a treadmill and no matter how fast we moved our feet, we didn't get any closer to the trees.

"Are they behind us?" Nora said without turning around. "They probably heard the gunshot. Damn it, damn it, damn it!"

I didn't want to turn around, but I did it anyway. If they were chasing us, it would be much better to have that information. I looked over my shoulder but I didn't see anyone behind us, and I didn't see piles of armed guards pouring out of every door.

"Nothing… no one," I said taking in a sharp breath. It wasn't until I breathed hard that I remembered my rib. When I wasn't thinking about it, I had been able to ignore the pain, but once I remembered it came back and it seared through my entire body. It wasn't going to let me forget, at least not for long.

My pace must have slowed because Nora glanced at me with worry filling her eyes. She was probably thinking about how if I didn't keep up with her, they'd eventually find us and take us back. Maybe she was thinking about how she'd keep running and leave me behind.

"They aren't back there," I said between my teeth, but I felt just as worried as she looked. I was trying to say something that would make me feel better too, but it hadn't worked.

"You don't know. They could be… they could be coming in cars or something," she said between quick breaths. "Come on, Ros! You have to keep moving!"

"I'm coming… I can do it," I said, but the words were for myself, not for her. I took a deep breath and started running again just as hard as I had when I had forgotten about the pain. I had to get the adrenaline going again so that maybe it wouldn't feel as though someone was sticking a blade between my bones.

We ran for as long as we could, until my legs were numb. My knees were threatening to give out if I took one more step. I just didn't have the same energy I had before my injury.

Nora stopped and turned towards me. I could tell her legs were feeling tired too, as they shifted slightly with each step she took. She looked unsteady as she reached out and placed her hand on a tree trunk.

It seemed as though we had made it… we had actually escaped. But I didn't want to get my hopes up. They could still be looking for us, but they just hadn't found us yet. We couldn't take a break. We couldn't stop moving.

"I think we should have thought this

through better," Nora said, her breathing erratic and heavy.

"What do you mean?"

"We have nothing but this gun… no food, no water. I'm back in the same exact situation I was in before they took me in. At least in there I had food." She looked as though she was starting to panic. Her mind was probably filling with images of how hard it really was out here fighting for your life.

Nora had almost died because she hadn't been eating before she came to the facility. But what she didn't know was that I could help.

"Don't worry. I can find us food… water too. We'll be OK, we just need to get further from that place. I have to find my way back."

"Back to where? You can't leave me alone out here!"

I shook my head. Nora had helped me… it wasn't like I was about to leave her behind. I'd have to figure out what I'd do, but we were a team. Penn and Carter would understand, at least I hoped they would once I told them what happened.

"I'm not going to leave you, but I am going to find my way back to the place I was at before being taken. If you want to join me you can, but that's where I'm going," I said as I started to walk slowly through the trees again while wrapping my arms around my stomach. My side was throbbing, and I was trying to do everything I could to hold myself together.

"I don't have anywhere better to go," she said taking a few steps to catch up with me. "Do I need to worry about where we're going? Do you even know where we are?

I looked around but all I could see were trees in every direction. I needed more information to help figure out where I was.

"You have nothing to worry about and I have no idea where we are. We need to find a marked road, a gas station, a house... something that might help us figure out where we are."

"Right," she said with a skip in her step. "And we need food too."

"Let's keep moving," I said as I carefully crouched down to the ground. I grabbed a handful of leaves that were barely still green and popped them into my mouth.

"Uh, are you sure you should eat that? What if it's poison?"

"What?"

Nora looked at me with wide eyes and pointed to my hand, "That... should you be eating that?"

"Oh! Yeah, it's fine. I can't remember what it's called, but it's edible," I said bending slowly and snatching up a few more leaves. Even though I was tempted to pop them into my own mouth, I held out my hand and offered them to Nora.

"Are you sure? Who told you this was safe?" Nora looked at me as though she wondered if I was playing a joke on her.

I shook my head, "A friend of mine. Just try them. You saw me eat them... I promise it's fine."

137

She took them and looked at them before she put them in her mouth. Nora barely took a bite, "Eww!" she said, looking as though she was struggling to swallow the bits down.

"Yeah, it's a little bitter… you'll get used to it," I said as I forced my feet to keep moving. "If we can't find a place to stay by nightfall, we'll have to find somewhere that looks safe enough where we can camp outside for the night."

* * *

I wasn't sure how long we had walked for when we came upon a house. It was small and secluded, and it seemed like a perfect place to hide out.

The only problem was I still didn't know where we were. We could have been walking in the complete opposite direction of the way I wanted to go, and with my pain that was the last thing I wanted to do.

"We can stay in there," I said nodding towards the house.

Nora seemed unsure about the idea but she didn't say no. She swallowed hard and took a deep breath.

"We'll just make sure it's empty," I said and Nora nodded. I didn't ask, but I figured she had done the same thing before the facility had found her.

Even though she seemed nervous, where

138

else would she have stayed, if not in a house? She took another deep breath as if trying to summon courage. But she didn't need courage, I'd seen her use the gun, I knew she'd do it again if it came down to it.

"Come on, it'll be fine," I said waving her along.

Nora pulled out the gun from her waistband and held it close to her body. We walked around the perimeter of the house and tried to look in the windows. Most of the curtains were closed, but based on what we could see, it seemed as though it had been abandoned.

When there didn't seem to be any signs of life, we approached the house from the backyard. I paused before we reached the back door and stared at the gun.

"What?" Nora said scrunching her eyebrows together.

"Is it even loaded?"

"I used it once." Nora shrugged and slid the top of the pistol back to reveal a bullet in the chamber. She grinned, "We have at least one."

"That's better than an empty gun," I said turning back towards the house. "Ready?"

When the gun made a tick, I turned back towards her. I raised my eyebrow and watched as she checked the magazine. She clearly was far more experienced with a gun than she had let on.

"What?" she asked when she noticed me staring at her.

"Nothing," I said wondering what other skills Nora had hidden up her sleeve. After all, she had shot that person back at the facility quickly and accurately. "You seem to know what you're doing with that thing."

She took in a quick breath, "Who said I didn't? I just never had to use one very much... especially on people."

I widened my eyes and opened my mouth, but closed it again. Everyone left in this world probably knew how to use a gun to some extent. I hadn't asked her a lot of questions about much of anything, but she could have offered up her experience level when we'd discussed our escape plan.

"We're good to go," she said and pointed the gun towards the ground, but I could tell by the look in her eyes that she was ready to put it up and use it if the situation called for it.

"How many were in there?"

"Enough, let's go," she said waiting for me to move.

I looked away and rolled my eyes as I grabbed the metal bar tighter. All I could do was trust that if something happened, she'd be able to land another bullet in the same exact spot I'd seen her hit once already.

I couldn't help but feel a little more curious about Nora. There was so much I didn't know about her. I had been too focused on leaving to find out more about Nora.

At the time, all that mattered to me was her eagerness to leave. I was very thankful for her help in escaping the facility. If it wasn't for her, I'd still be inside.

My hand reached out to twist the doorknob, and I wasn't surprised to find it unlocked. I pushed it open and stepped back waiting for bullets to come flying out of the door, but they didn't. The only thing I heard was the squeaky hinges of the door as it swayed back and forth slightly in the light breeze.

I tipped my head to the side. Nora caught my order and stepped to the other side of the door. She peeked inside from her angle and nodded before stepping inside of the house.

I followed her and closed the door behind us, turning only slightly to flip the lock into place. Nora moved around the room, shifting her gun this way and that, as if she was a trained police officer looking for an intruder.

I held my metal bar up, but if there was someone inside, I wasn't sure what good my hunk of metal would be to protect either of us. It would only be helpful if we came across someone who was completely unarmed, which wasn't likely. Ever since the storms, it seemed as though this was a way of life. Everyone was armed. Not because they wanted to be, but because they had to be.

Nora and I finished checking the house in record time. Her systematic methods were quick and efficient. She seemed to be just as good at thoroughly checking a house as Penn was, if not slightly better.

"Empty," she said as if I hadn't realized that no one had jumped out and shot at us. "Lock the doors and check the windows to make sure everything is locked up tight."

It irked me how she was bossing me around. She went from seeming to be unsure, to being some kind of expert.

None of it probably mattered since she was right about what to do. If we were going to stay the night, we had to make sure the house was secured and that it would stay that way.

We split up the rooms to check the locks. Nora took the side with the kitchen and I took the side with the bedrooms.

The house was so small that it didn't take long for me to check the windows. I wasn't surprised that everything was locked up tight. Whoever had lived here before the storms probably locked up, thinking that they'd be back.

After I finished, Nora was standing in the kitchen already going through the cabinets. I watched her as she looked. I shivered at the coldness in the empty house.

Nora opened one of the cabinets and pulled down a box of toaster pastries. She set them down on the counter and looked at me with a smile on her face.

When I didn't move fast enough she shrugged and peeled the cardboard box open. She pulled out a package and ripped the wrapper open with her teeth.

After she took a large bite, she pushed the box of sugary breakfast treats towards me and raised a brow. She slammed down a large bottle of water on the top of the counter.

"Oh and I found water too," she said as she finished the pastry.

I stepped closer and grabbed myself a package. I twisted off the top of the water bottle and closed my eyes as I took a long, slow drink of the cool liquid.

When I put the bottle back down and started to push it towards her, she put her palm out and shook her head. Nora held up another bottle, "I found two."

I couldn't help but smile at the amount of water I had all to myself. Even in the facility the water had been carefully rationed, but here, in the middle of nowhere, I had a big bottle all to myself.

Nora bent down and opened one of the lower cabinets. She stepped to the side and revealed the contents, "I guess I found more than two."

Inside the cabinet were rows and rows of bottles of water. I didn't know if I should laugh or cry.

"It's so beautiful," I said pretending to wipe away a tear.

"Maybe we should just stay here," she said taking a drink from her bottle.

I shook my head. "You're more than welcome to stay, but I have to keep going."

"Oh, that's right. Whatever you have out there waiting for you," she said raising an eyebrow.

I took a bite from the toaster pastry so I wouldn't have to say anything. I still didn't know how much I should tell her about what was out there for me. If she'd be joining me at our little place in Michigan, at some point I'd have to tell her about it. Maybe she wouldn't even want to come with me.

"What was that?" Nora said spinning around quickly to face the back door.

I narrowed my eyes and shook my head. I hadn't heard anything. I stared at the locked door hoping it would make anyone who might be out there change their mind and leave.

We were armed. Even if there was someone on the other side and they entered, we'd have the upper-hand. At least that's what I had to hope.

When I heard the sound of a key being inserted into the metal lock my heart started to pound against my chest so loudly I was sure that whoever was on the other side of the door could hear it. I placed my hand over it as though I was trying to muffle the sounds.

"Oh shit, come on," Nora whispered as she grabbed our water bottles and led the way towards the front door. I thought she was going to open it and make a run for it, but instead she opened the closet and stepped inside.

At the same time the back door opened, Nora pulled me inside the closet and closed the door soundlessly. I shivered when a large man entered the house. He growled out a sigh and dropped a backpack on the floor.

Somehow I knew without a single doubt that this was his home. We were trapped inside the closet of his house.

Chapter sixteen.

My eyes refused to blink. I didn't want to take my eyes off of the man for even a second.

My breathing was short and each breath was so sharp it stung my chest. It felt as though the closet walls were starting to close in around us, and even though I wanted to scream, I couldn't.

The door had small decorative slits cut into it at about eye level which allowed Nora and me to keep our eyes on the man. As long as he was in the kitchen, dining area or living room, we would be able to see him.

My body felt stiff, and I worried that Nora or I would make a small noise that would alert him to the fact that something was off in his home. I didn't even want to shift my weight, I was so worried that a floorboard would creak.

He put down a rifle next to the backpack he had set down and let out a deep breath. He pushed the curtain on the backdoor so he could look out the window. It seemed as though he was looking for something… or someone. His head quickly shifted back towards the kitchen as he let the curtain fall back into place.

Before moving, he tilted his head to the side as though he'd noticed something was amiss, but then he grunted and dragged his feet towards the kitchen cabinets. If he noticed something, apparently it wasn't enough to investigate further. Or maybe he was just too hungry and thirsty to care.

What I hadn't considered when we first found this house was that the reason it was so well stocked was because someone was still living in it. I was pretty sure if he found out someone had been, scratch that, *was* still inside of his house, he wouldn't be too happy about it. Surely he wouldn't want to share his precious supplies.

This guy wasn't going to leave anytime soon. It could be days, maybe weeks. We had no way to know.

Panic started to set in and I was having trouble controlling my breathing. If I didn't slow it down and keep myself quiet, he was definitely going to find us.

When the back door opened and a second man noisily entered the house my breathing stopped completely. Or at least that was how it felt.

Things had gone from bad to worse in a blink of an eye. I didn't know how many bullets were in the gun Nora had, but I hoped it was enough.

I slowly raised my arm, hoping my joints wouldn't squeak as I placed my hand tightly over my own mouth. My stomach twisted in a tight knot threatening to throw whatever was inside of my belly out.

Nora must have been able to sense the change in my body language, or in my breathing. I turned to see her looking at me with eyes just as wide as mine were. The light from the slits in the

146

door made her eyes glow with a haunting, yellow brightness. Her face was striped with thin lines of light that made her look like a wild animal.

"What... is... it?" she said, mostly mouthing the words.

"Him," I said through a small opening between my fingers. I looked back and forth between the two men as though I was sure they had heard me, but neither of them made any indication that they had.

Nora looked at me, shaking her head. I knew she wasn't understanding who he was or why I was silently freaking out.

"He's the one," I breathed slowly, "that almost killed me."

"Oh crap," she mouthed and sucked in a silent breath of air, keeping her body still.

If he got his hands on me again, I knew I wouldn't survive. Not just because I was hiding in his house, but because I had escaped the first time. He would want to finish what he had started. The man would break every bone in my body before he finished me off too.

My fist tightened trying to grab onto the metal bar in case I needed to use it, but that was when I realized something was wrong. I no longer had the metal bar. I looked through the cracks in the door and saw it sitting on the kitchen counter up against the wall where I had left it.

My breathing was rapid and I couldn't take my eyes off of the bar. It was as though I was trying to make it disappear. The light from the windows hit the silver-colored bar in just the right

147

way that it practically made it sparkle. It was like it wanted to be noticed.

"Where have you been?" the beefy man said to the one that had attacked me. "Catch any?"

The man that had attacked me grunted and unzipped his heavy brown jacket. "Nothing. How about you?"

"Nahhh," the beefy man said, dragging out the word. He pulled out a pack of cigarettes and tapped them against the top of the kitchen counter. The beefy man flicked the box and grabbed the one that stuck out of the pack the furthest with his lips. He looked around the room as he clicked his lighter and lit the cigarette.

The one that had attacked me dropped his things down to the floor, walked around the counter and into the kitchen. My attacker bent down behind the counter and, even though I couldn't see what he was doing, I knew he was opening the cabinet that contained their water supply.

"Jesus, Chris!" my attacker shouted as he slammed the cabinet door shut.

"What?" the beefy man said looking angry and confused.

"Take it easy on the water, would you?" the one that had attacked me said, standing up. His eyes shifted around as though he could tell something wasn't right. It felt as though his gaze settled right on the closet… right on me.

The one, Chris, stood in front of him blocking the closet from his view. Chris stretched out his fingers on his right hand and tightened them into a fist. I couldn't see either of their faces, but I assumed they were staring at one another.

It must have just been my imagination that my attacker had been looking in my direction because if he had, he would have done something or said something, but he hadn't. My attacker walked away from Chris, roughly hitting him with his shoulder.

His boots clacked against the floor as he walked out of the kitchen. Chris turned around to glare at him.

"You know what? Fuck you, Marv," Chris said looking into the cabinet. "We have more than enough and it's easy enough to get more. In fact, I'll refill again before I leave."

If Chris noticed any of the bottles were missing, he didn't say anything. I had to hope that the men didn't keep a running inventory of their supplies, and if they did, they would blame the missing water bottles on the other.

The man that had attacked me, Marv, plopped down in a chair at the dining room table and twisted open his bottle of water. He drank nearly half of the bottle in one drink before he set it down and slowly spun the plastic cap back on top.

Marv looked up and noticed Chris staring at him. He grunted, "What?"

"You run into those kids again?"

"Nah… I don't see them very often. Three times total, maybe? That day was just a day filled with bad luck," Marv said.

Chris laughed, "You were scared off by a couple of dumb kids."

Marv snarled as his eyebrows shifted

downward, "Dumb, armed kids. The most dangerous kind."

"Come on... you couldn't handle a few kids? Bet I could have."

"I'm sure I could have if they hadn't taken me by surprise. I will get them if they come through here again. Why are we even talking about this?" Marv said sounding agitated as he pressed his fists down on the tabletop.

"What do you want to talk about?" Chris asked with an annoying laugh.

"What's for dinner?"

Chris walked into the kitchen and opened one of the top cabinets. He pulled out a can of soup and held it out for Marv's approval. When Marv nodded, he tossed him the can.

"Chunky again?"

"So many options these days, huh? Feel free to make yourself something better," Chris said as he took out his own can and grabbed two spoons from one of the drawers. "So, when are you heading back out?"

"Soon as I finish this," Marv said nodding towards the can. "You?"

Chris shook his head side to side, "Not sure, need to rebuild my strength."

Marv chuckled as he grabbed a spoon from his buddy and pulled open the top of the soup can. "I have to do all of the work, huh?"

"Oh come on," Chris said slamming his fist down causing the spoon and can to rattle. "We barely even come across any trespassers anymore. We should just be done... wait for them to come around here and deal with it when they do."

Marv stared at him.

"It's going to be winter soon. Snow and stuff."

Marv's eyes narrowed and I could see the evil in them. He shook his head and scooped the thick, cold soup into his mouth. "Wait for them to sneak up on us in our sleep and get us? Don't be stupid. Kill or be killed. That's the world we live in now."

"That girl wouldn't have harmed a fly," Chris said with a huff.

"Everyone is a threat and must be dealt with appropriately. If we don't police our territory who will? The more you open your mouth against me, the more I think you might be one of them," Marv said staring at Chris. After a long, uncomfortable pause he laughed, "Aw, I'm just kidding. We're in this together. Right, Chris?"

Chris blinked and then nodded, "What about when that place down south takes over, then what are we going to? Lot more of them then there are us. How are we going to protect our territory then?" He set his spoon down on the table and crossed his arms while he waited for a response.

"Still working out a plan for that. Blow it up or something."

Were they talking about the facility? I couldn't make much of their conversation other than it sounded like they were going to extremes to protect their territory.

Marv's spoon clinked as it scraped the bottom of the soup can. He raised the last scoop up

151

to his mouth and dropped the spoon down into the can. He leaned back on the back two legs of his chair.

"As long as we keep this area safe… we stay safe. It's that simple. Don't lose sight of our purpose, because the second you let your guard down, you put us both, and our home, in danger."

Chris nodded, but then he looked down, "Most people seem to just want to pass through. Don't seem to pay us much mind… hate doing what we do when they are just minding—"

"Are you saying you've just let people go?"

"No, of course not, but I don't go out of my way. I stay in our territory… I just wonder if maybe there is a better way," Chris said, and it looked as though he was suddenly regretting his words. "We're gone for days at a time policing our land. The things we do feel more like offense, rather than playing defense. I thought we were doing this just to keep ourselves, our stuff and our home safe. Sometimes when they look at me with those big, round doe eyes… well, it feels like I'm doing the wrong thing, Marv!"

"You're doing what you have to do. For us," Marv said as he reached over and rested his thick hand on Chris's shoulder. "We are doing what we have to do. Do you want to die?"

"Of course not," Chris said grabbing the empty soup cans off of the table. He tossed them into the trash and leaned back against the kitchen counter. "I'm just real tired is all."

Marv stood up and walked over to stand in front of him. He looked into his eyes, "Are you done with this all?" He waved his arm around indicating the house, "Are you going to give this all up?"

"No," Chris said sternly but turned away facing the closet that held Nora and me. My heart thumped hard.

"Kill them. Put them in the tree. That's all you have to do. You're finding someone once a week? Maybe every two weeks? It's working. We are winning. We can't stop now," Marv said moving his hand behind his back so that Chris couldn't see it. He tightened his hand into a hard fist. "If you have a problem with any of this… doubts or anything, it's time to fess up."

"I'm fine. I'm good, really I am," he said looking as though he knew if he answered wrong Marv would do something. "I just need sleep. It's not the protecting, it's just all the traveling and lack of sleep. I don't sleep so good when I'm out there," Chris said bowing his head.

After a few seconds, Marv's fist relaxed, "Me either, man. Rest my friend. Take your time, get your head back on straight. I'm heading out. I'll be gone several days… I have a lead on something. When you're up to it, go south, check out the place… get any wanderers."

Chris nodded. Marv stared at him for a few seconds before he smiled and slapped his friend on the back.

He grabbed his jacket and slipped it on. Marv took his pack into the kitchen and filled it with various items before he stood in front of the back door. He grabbed his rifle and saluted Chris before he left the house.

Chris stared at the door for a moment before his shoulders slumped down and he let out a sigh. He seemed relieved.

I wasn't exactly sure what the men were doing, but it sounded as though they were methodically patrolling their area, collecting supplies and killing anyone they came across whether they got in the way or not. The only thing I was sure of was that Nora and I needed to get out of here as soon as we could.

The man grabbed a rag from one of the drawers. He went to the table and wiped it clean before going back into the kitchen and wiping the counters. His hand swiped back and forth, each time inching closer to the metal bar, but he never seemed to notice it.

The crumbs sprinkled down to the ground as he shook out the towel. He grabbed a broom and started sweeping. After he dumped out the dustpan into the trash, he put the broom away and walked into the living room.

He was only a few feet away from where we were hiding in the closet. If he came over and opened the closet, there wouldn't be anything we could do but stare back at him.

Nora slowly raised the gun up to her chest and pointed it at the closet door. When he flopped down onto the sofa, she slowly lowered it back down. He tipped his head back and let out a big yawn.

It wasn't long before his mouth dropped downward and his chest moved slowly up and down with his relaxed breaths. He was so tired he fell asleep while sitting. Although, if he heard anything out of the ordinary, I was positive he would wake up.

My legs were starting to feel stiff and tired. I didn't know how much longer I could stand there pretending to be a statue.

He snorted abruptly and looked around. His eyes were wide, but then he blinked a few times before he stretched his arms up towards the ceiling.

He stood with a groan and walked like a zombie out of the room. It wasn't long before Nora and I heard his loud snoring coming from one of the bedrooms.

"Let's get out of here," Nora said gesturing towards the doorknob.

"We should wait," I said nervous we would wake him.

She nodded. We waited another five minutes or so before she reached out in front of me and carefully opened the door. Her fingers were shaking and I could tell she wanted to get out of the closet just as badly as I did, maybe even more.

I stepped out and watched for the man to come out, but he didn't. Nora started slowly walking towards the kitchen... away from the front door.

"Nora!" I said quickly in a hushed voice. "What are you doing?"

"Water," she said, and I watched as she moved across the floor silently. I twisted my fingers against one another as I waited for her.

She'd made it to the kitchen and bent down

at the same moment I heard footsteps stomping down the short hallway. He stopped at the end of the hall and looked at me with a terrifying smirk on his face.

Chapter seventeen.

I wanted to scream or run, but I was frozen in place. It felt as though I had become an ice sculpture, only with a look of sheer terror on my face. I couldn't force the words out to warn Nora.

"I knew something was up when I saw that bar on the counter," he said tilting his head towards the kitchen. "You here alone?"

I nodded, but he didn't look as though he believed it. He kept his eyes glued to me as he walked backwards towards the kitchen.

When I saw his gun resting against the wall, I knew what he was doing. There wasn't anything I could do to stop him. I didn't even have the metal bar to defend myself with, not that it would have helped at all against the rifle.

"This must be my lucky day," he said looking me up and down. "How did you get in here anyway?"

I shook my head still too frightened to speak, but I knew Nora was hearing everything and she was the one with the gun. She would have to be the one to save us.

If I tried to run, I was sure he'd catch me. And if I didn't try to run, I was sure he was going to kill me. Either way, if one of us didn't come up with something, I was going to be killed.

He glanced towards the kitchen but Nora

must have been well-hidden because he turned back to face me. "You going to make me ask again? I don't like to ask things twice," he said with a small frown.

"You don't have to do this," I said thinking back to how he had told Marv he wasn't sure if they were doing the right thing.

"Of course I do. You're in my home."

"You could just let me go. I was just passing through, I didn't know anyone lived here," I said shaking my head.

"How. Did. You. Get. In. Here?" he said clenching his teeth together.

My eyes widened when I saw Nora pop up and point the gun directly at the man. He must have noticed her movement out of the corner of his eye because he quickly lifted his gun, but he was slower than Nora.

She pulled the trigger and hit him right between the eyes. It was the same spot she'd hit the girl who tried to stop us from leaving the facility. Her accuracy with that pistol was amazing.

"The door was open, dumbass," she said as his body slumped to the ground. Blood oozed from of his wound and poured out onto the floor.

"Oh crap," I whispered as words finally found the way out of my mouth. I took several quick steps towards the front door and grabbed the doorknob.

Nora was already at my side putting her hand over mine to stop me from opening the door. She peeked out of the window before letting go of my hand.

"In case the other one is out there," she whispered.

I nodded and then turned the knob. I stepped out of the house and ran without bothering to look back. Nora's footsteps didn't sound as though they were too far behind, but I didn't turn around to check.

I ran as fast as I could until the pain in my side started to spread through my entire body. It was surprising that my body was still working after everything I'd been through.

"Why are we running?" Nora said between breaths. "He's dead!"

I kept moving until her words registered. "The other one could have heard the gunshot," I said as I slowed my feet... not because I wanted to but because I had to. My eyes darted around as I looked to make sure we weren't being followed.

The last thing I wanted was for my attacker to be chasing us, or maybe it wouldn't be a terrible thing. If he had followed us, Nora would probably be able to put a bullet between his eyes too. Then I wouldn't have to worry about running into him ever again.

"We should keep moving," I said looking around as I spun in a slow circle. "We don't even know if there were only two of them in their psycho club. There could be more of them!"

"OK," Nora said looking at the horizon where the sun was quickly lowering, turning the sky a shade of red that reminded me of the color of blood. "Which way?"

I looked in the direction of the setting sun.

If I was looking west I knew we wanted to head north… the facility had been located to the south, but I didn't even know for sure if we were still in Michigan. I crossed my fingers and nodded in the direction I thought was north.

Nora walked next to me and I could tell something was bothering her. She kept looking back towards the fully stocked house we had left behind.

"What?" I said without looking at her.

"We should have taken that rifle. And as much water as we could carry." She kicked at a stone on the ground so hard it flew through the air and hit a tree trunk.

She was right. We should have taken the gun, but all I could think about was getting out of there. For all we knew the other one, Marv, was still close enough that he could have made it back while we were packing up supplies. Or he could have been waiting outside.

"I'm not sure it was worth the risk. We have a gun, and we can find food and water, let's just get out of here," I said picking up my pace as much as my wrecked, sore body would allow.

We were quickly losing sunlight, and I knew we didn't want to, nor could we easily, travel at night. We were going to have to find somewhere to stop and camp for the night.

Only about five minutes passed before I pointed to a small grouping of trees that looked as though it would keep us hidden. Nora followed me.

Once we got to the trees, I stepped inside the tight grouping and looked around to see how well we'd be hidden. It would have to do. I only wished the trees and bushes would have been more lush.

Nora stood there watching me as I rearranged a pile of leaves. I sat down on them with my back to one of the trees and winced when I tried to hug my knees to my chest for warmth.

"All that running didn't help?" Nora said with a small smile.

"Ha," I said shivering, as the night air somehow felt even colder near the ground. I cupped my hands around my mouth and breathed into them.

Nora looked through the trees, her eyes stopping at a clearing off to the side, "Is this really the best spot? Anyone coming through will see a fire."

"What fire?" I said rubbing my hands together.

"Oh," Nora grunted not bothering to hide her disappointment. "When we were out, we always had a fire."

A fire would have been nice, but if Marv passed by it would have probably meant certain death for the both of us. And it wasn't limited to just Marv, for all we knew there were others out there like him. Or worse. HOME. The resistance. Wendy and her friends looking for us to take us back to the facility. The more we stayed out of sight, the more likely it would be that I'd make it back to Penn and Carter.

Nora sat down next to me and wrapped her arms easily around her thin legs, "Now what do we do?"

"We take turns sleeping. As soon as we get some sunlight, we can move again." My stomach rumbled and Nora looked at me. I had gotten used to the frequent meals in the facility, but it seemed as though my stomach hadn't gotten the memo that we'd left. We were back to eating when we could find food. I knew I'd adjust.

"Hungry?"

"Yes, but I'll be fine." I'd done this before, and from what she'd told me, she had too. Hopefully her body would be able to handle it for the time being.

In the morning we'd find food and water. I felt confident that I'd be able to find something, but it would have to wait. First, we had to make it through the night.

We sat in silence. I think we were both watching the moon rise high into the air, glowing brightly as the sky around it grew darker.

"Why don't you sleep first. We'll sleep in shifts," I said looking at the little reflection from the moon that sparkled in her eyes. I wished I could look deep enough that I could learn everything about her with just one look.

"You should sleep first, really I don't mind," Nora said looking away from me.

The blood was still pumping through my veins from having seen my attacker again so close up. I just felt more comfortable taking the first shift myself. If he was coming, I wanted to be the one that spotted him. I shook my head, "Not tired yet, please, I insist."

162

"If you're sure—"

"I'm sure."

Nora sighed and lowered her body to the ground. She curled up into a small ball, turning on her side so her back was to me, but she kept her body close.

"Nora?"

She twisted her head to the side slightly, "Yeah?"

"I need the gun," I whispered as I looked at it in the back of her pants. When she fell asleep I could have taken it, but I decided to just ask.

"Oh right, of course," she said as she removed the gun and stretched her arm back towards me. She didn't even bother to turn around.

"Thanks," I said wrapping my fingers around the cold metal. Hopefully, I wouldn't have to use it because I knew I couldn't hit my target as accurately as Nora would be able to.

I'd seen her in action and I knew she was a much better shot. Maybe she'd had more practice before, or maybe even after the storms. I'd ask her about it in the morning.

After about ten minutes, Nora was in a deep sleep. I watched her body rise slowly with each breath and then sink back down as she exhaled. It was kind of hypnotic.

Nora didn't know much about me but she seemed trusting from the start. She followed me out into the unknown, when pretty much all I told her was that I had been attacked. Maybe she felt as though she didn't have a choice, since she wanted to get out too.

163

I wondered what Penn and Carter would think about her once they met her. If they met her. What choice did I have? I couldn't just leave her out here to fend for herself.

It was on my third shift when I heard them in the distance. The dog-beasts and their haunting howls were something I could easily recognize. They were around, but they sounded very far away.

Their cries were frightening to hear, but as long as I could hear them I could tell that, for the time being, they were far enough away. We weren't in immediate danger, at least for now.

I'd almost forgotten about them, but they were still out there. Day or night, the dog-beasts were still hunting their prey.

I shivered so abruptly that it woke Nora. The moon had made its way across the sky. I hadn't gotten much rest, but I knew morning was on the way and I was anxious to get moving.

Nora sat up and stretched her arms over her head. The second the sun moved a centimeter over the horizon, I stood up and brushed off my clothing.

I cleared my throat and took a step away from the trees out into the clearing. I looked around and then back at Nora, "Let's go."

Chapter eighteen.

My body didn't want to move easily. I was frozen from the cold and my legs felt stiff from all the previous day's running. My side was screaming at me, but ever since they'd stopped giving me the pain relievers back at the facility, it had become easier for me to push through the pain.

Now that we were out, I could look for medicine. Maybe I would be able to find something that would help take the edge off so we could move even faster.

At first we walked slowly. It felt like we'd been walking forever, but we weren't making any progress. Both Nora and I were exhausted from everything we'd been through. Our few hours of sleep hadn't helped nearly enough.

Nora stepped in front of me and pulled some leaves out of the ground. They were mostly brown with weird reddish spots… it looked like they were diseased, or dead.

She turned to me and held them up inches from my face, "Are these edible?"

"Uh, I don't think so," I said shaking my head and trying not to laugh. For all I knew they were, but they didn't look like anything Carter had ever shown me before.

She tossed them to the ground and the gun in the back of her waistband caught my eye. I

165

reached behind me even though I knew I wouldn't find the gun there.

"When did you get the gun back?" I said trying to remember. I had taken the last shift and I could have sworn I had the gun.

"Huh?" Nora said reaching behind her back. It looked like she was just as surprised to find it there. "I guess I never gave it back to you after my last shift."

We both had been very tired. It was possible we could have forgotten to switch back, but I could almost remember holding the gun before the sun came up.

"I guess not," I said taking a deep breath. The sun was a bit higher in the sky and I could finally feel its warmth against me. The air was still cool, but the sun was penetrating my skin, working to warm my chilled bones.

"Hey! Look!" Nora said pointing to an old country road that cut a path through a sparse patch of trees. The road didn't appear to be in great condition, even back before the storms it wouldn't have been anything that had heavy traffic, but it was something. There was a chance this road could take us to a town, near some homes, or maybe it would just lead to a dead end. But it was better than wandering around practically aimlessly.

Nora started walking towards it waving anxiously for me to follow, "Come on! What are you waiting for?"

"We usually didn't stay on the roads," I said and she stuck her tongue out at me. "Whatever, just seems smarter to me," I mumbled so quietly I knew she wouldn't have been able to hear me.

"No one is going to be traveling out here... when is the last time you even saw a car?"

"When Wendy and the others put me in one and drove me to their stupid facility," I said trying to replay the event in my mind, but I couldn't. Too much was missing.

If only I could remember a sign post or some kind of landmark, but I couldn't think of a single thing I'd seen along the way that might help me get back to Penn and Carter. I just needed to find something, so I would know I was leading us in the right direction.

Nora smiled, "So, not very often then. We'll be fine, come on."

I looked around as though I expected a car to come barreling down the road, but of course, there wasn't one. The road was desolate except for the sound of our footsteps scraping against the crumbling pavement and an occasional tweet from a hiding bird.

I couldn't even guess how long we had walked when a beat-up sign came into view. The city name that had once been there was now spray-painted over, but the bold number five was still there.

"Five miles!" Nora said sounding excited. "We'll be there in no time."

"Wherever *there* is," I said worried that there might be a reason the city name had been vandalized. Maybe it was a sign that we shouldn't have been heading into the city.

I didn't think we had much of a choice. We

167

were hungry, thirsty and most of all, I needed to figure out where I was. It wasn't like we could wander around forever just hoping to stumble upon something that would help me figure out exactly where we were. What I needed was a map.

When we finally walked into the city, it was like we had walked right into a ghost town in an old wild west movie. It felt like the town was completely abandoned, but at the same time it felt like there were hundreds of eyes on us… watching… waiting.

"There," Nora said pointing down the street.

The building she indicated had once been a gas station. Someone must not have been happy when they stopped here because all of the pumps looked as though they had a thorough beating, likely with a sledgehammer. The building was covered in overgrown vines and looked as though it was coated with a fine layer of dirt.

The gas station didn't look like it had been entered in ages, which was hopefully a good thing. Even if everything had been looted, maybe, at the very least, we could figure out where we were.

We walked up to the building, and I noticed a clear spot on the dirt covered window. It looked as though someone had come up to the building, not that long ago, and pressed their hand into the dirt making a nearly perfect handprint. Nora reached out to open the door, but I quickly pulled her arm back.

I pointed at the hand print and she narrowed her eyes at me. She raised her eyebrow and lip as though she didn't know what the fuss was about.

"Just hold on a second," I said as I stood on my tip-toes and peered inside the building. "Hmm, OK. I don't see anything. Go ahead."

Nora rolled her eyes at me and tried to push open the door, but it barely moved.

"Is it locked?"

"I don't think so. Give me a hand," she said and we both pushed as hard as we could. The door moved slowly, squeaking horrifically with every inch we managed to move it. We stopped when there was enough room for the both of us to sneak inside, one after the other.

"Cool," Nora said looking around the partially filled gas station. She held out her arms and walked backwards, showcasing everything that had been left behind. I was surprised by how much was still on the shelves.

"It's probably all expired," I said with a grunt.

Nora started sifting through the items on the shelves while I wandered around. The place was quiet. It was eerie to hear nothing, except for the infrequent rustling noises from Nora. There was no hum of electricity, no sounds of traffic outside the four walls, nothing. Everything was completely silent.

On the back wall, under a sign with an arrow that pointed to the restrooms, was a faded map of the state. I smiled. We were still in Michigan.

I placed my finger over the little sticker that indicated where in Michigan we were. My eyes quickly shifted upwards as I scanned the map trying

169

to find where Penn and Carter were hopefully waiting for me. When I saw the distance we still had to cover, by foot, I wanted to cry. We still had a long way to go.

"We're still in Michigan," I shouted across the room. My words echoed sharply in the emptiness of the gas station.

"That's good… are we far from where you want to go?" I could hear Nora ripping open a package.

"Yeah," I said, repeatedly tracing a line on the map from where we were to where we needed to go.

"How far?"

I bit my finger as I tried to figure out how long it would take us to get there. But I wasn't sure I could even make an accurate guess… it was going to take longer than I wanted, that much I knew. "Far. Days… maybe weeks? I have no idea."

"Oh, here," she said popping up from behind one of the shelving units. The second I turned around she tossed a package to me.

I caught it, and I could feel the little raisins moving inside the box. "Thanks," I said pinching the cardboard and ripping the box open. I poured too many of them into my mouth making it hard to chew them at first. I didn't even realize how hungry I was until the sweet little raisins touched my tongue.

"The good news is that we were at least sort of traveling in the right direction," I said finishing the second half of the box.

If she heard me, she didn't respond. Nora

walked behind the counter and pulled out a plastic bag from under the dusty register. She walked back to the shelf, and I could tell by the sounds that she was putting the boxes of raisins into the plastic bag.

"What?" she said when she noticed me watching her.

"Find anything anything with vitamins that we can take?" I said walking over to join her. I glanced at the shelf but the only items left on that particular one were the bagged snacks, prepackaged donuts and stuffed mini-cakes that were all likely beyond their expiration date.

"Not yet," she said opening another box and popping some of the raisins into her mouth. "Now what?" she said, her voice muffled by the food.

"Save some... who knows when or if we'll find more," I said with a shrug.

Nora told me that when she arrived at the facility, she had been starving to death. It seemed odd to me that someone who had often went without food wouldn't be more careful to ration it. To me it seemed she was acting more like someone who wasn't used to going without food for long stretches of time. But what did I know?

"Of course," she said as she slowed her chewing. "I'm not stupid. Just really hungry."

I walked around the counter and grabbed my own plastic bag. I walked around the gas station looking at the shelves I didn't think Nora had checked yet.

Inside one of the non-working coolers sat three bottles of water staring back at me. The water inside the clear plastic sparkled and tried to tempt me into drinking them. I stuffed them into my bag and turned around to find several cans of soup on the shelf behind me.

On another shelf, I found two packs of bandages and some pain relievers that were still in a sealed package. There were probably other things that we could have taken, but my nerves were starting to get the better of me. I couldn't think straight and I wanted to get moving. I was ready to get back on the road to start on the long journey to Penn and Carter.

"We should go," I said walking back towards the front door. The windows were so dirty I couldn't see through them, but I could tell the sun was disappearing.

I spun around, unable to blink as I connected eyes with Nora. She was wearing a stunned expression. Nora must have noticed the change in lighting. It was still day... the sky should not have been turning dark. She blinked, breaking our locked gaze, and then spun in a slow circle, "What's going on?"

Something in the air changed. And I didn't like it.

"I'm not sure."

I stepped over to the window where the handprint was and peered out of the small cleaned area. The sky above us was so dark it was almost black. There was a storm coming.

"Crap," I said rubbing my palm over my closed eyes. I didn't want to be stuck here any longer than we had to be, but when I saw a bolt of lightning zip down and crack the earth, I knew we

172

didn't have a choice. "A storm."

"A storm? What kind of storm?"

"Not sure," I said as the rain started to tap loudly against the windows and the roof.

A low rumble of thunder erupted and rolled for more than a minute. It felt like the ground under my feet was vibrating.

"Guess we're stuck here until it passes," I said peering out of the small, clean handprint. There wasn't more than a few seconds between each of the lightning strikes, as the storm rapidly drew nearer. They flashed down and touched the earth with a frequency I'd only ever seen once before.

We were lucky to be inside the gas station. We wouldn't have been safe out there. Then again, I wasn't exactly sure we'd be safe inside the gas station either.

The ground was almost constantly shaking under my feet and shelving units rattled at the same time. Nora stood there staring towards the dirty windows looking terrified, but she wouldn't have been able to see anything but random flashes of light.

"I hate storms," she said wrapping her arms around her middle.

"Yeah."

"No, I really hate storms," she said looking at me with wide eyes.

"You and me both," I said remembering the storm that had taken everything away. Maybe she was thinking about it too. The storm that had changed all of our lives forever, flinging us into a world I still couldn't comprehend.

I was about to ask Nora about what things had been like for her in the big storm when something hit the top of the roof with a loud bang. It sounded as though a boulder had been dropped on the roof. I backed away and stared up at the ceiling.

"What the hell was that?" Nora said in a panicked, shrieking voice.

Then another hit the roof, harder. I stopped myself from screaming.

My mind flashed back to the lethal chunks of hail I'd seen fall so long ago. Was it happening again? Was this storm going to wipe the Earth of anything that had been left behind after the first time?

I'd die in this gas station, never seeing Penn or Carter again. Penn would somehow survive. He'd find a way.

The hail hit against the roof rapidly. It was so loud I had to cover my ears. I was surprised it wasn't crashing through the roof.

I stepped up to look out of the clean handprint in the glass, but screamed when a chunk of hail broke through the glass about two feet to my right. Then another slammed through the far end of the window, crashing to the floor.

The rounded piece of hail that came through the window near me had broken into four smaller pieces. I hadn't gotten a good look, but if I would have put all the pieces back together, it would have been slightly larger than the size of a softball.

"Ros!" Nora yelled over the noises of the

storm. I knew she was calling for me, but I couldn't move. Another broke through just to my left. "Get away from the window!"

I lifted my left hand up and saw the wet blood drip down my wrist. A stray shard of glass must have cut me. Even when another chunk of hail broke through the window just above my head, I still couldn't make my feet work. I felt the bits of glass rain down on top of my head.

Nora shouted something, but I couldn't understand what she was saying. She sounded as though she was getting further away.

I looked up through the broken glass at the hypnotizing, black swirling clouds. They were calling for me.

It was my turn. All I had to do was walk out there and it would be done. I wouldn't have to struggle anymore. They would take me to the others.

I took a step towards the door and reached out for the handle.

Chapter nineteen.

Nora grabbed me around the middle and pulled me back. She was maneuvering me around the shelves towards the back corner of the gas station near the bathrooms.

"Are you crazy?" she shrieked in a high-pitched voice. It looked like she was ready to slap me across the face.

"I-ah, umm." I didn't know what to say. She probably wouldn't even understand if I told her everything I'd been through. Everyone I'd lost and missed terribly.

"Don't do that again!"

We both sunk down to the ground. There weren't any windows in the area, but it wasn't a large gas station, if the storm wanted us, it could take us.

All I could hear was the sound of the hail hitting the roof and glass breaking, as my stomach pulsed with each boom of thunder. It felt as though all hope was being pounded out of my body.

I was imagining the tornadoes swirling around in the distance, laughing as they danced and twirled towards me. They hadn't taken me the first time, but this time they were determined. They weren't going to let me go.

I hugged my knees to my chest even though it made the pain in my side throb. Nora's body was tight against mine. Her body shook with each lightning strike and crash of thunder.

She was holding on to me so tightly that it seemed as though she was afraid to let go. As if she was worried that if she let go she'd be pulled right out of the gas station and into the storm.

"Oh God," she cried out as a gust of wind whistled through the gas station. It was so strong it whipped our hair around our faces and out towards the broken windows. "We're going to die!"

Another gust of wind whooshed through the gas station, blowing things around the room before sucking them out through the windows. It was hard to breath. The storm was pulling all of the oxygen out of what remained of the gas station.

My chest felt tight. It felt like someone was sitting on it… crushing me.

Another abnormally strong wind came through the room and pulled Nora and me slightly along the dirty tiled floor. I held onto Nora and pressed my feet against one of the shelving units to stop us from moving any further.

The winds pushed and pulled at us as though they were playing tug of war with Nora and me. A cacophony of deafening noises from the rain, hail, screeching winds, thunder and the shouts and screams that came out of Nora, filled the room.

When I thought it was too much and I couldn't hold us in place a second longer, the storm stopped. It was gone. There was no more wind. There was no more rain or hail. The noises, for the most part, were done, although I could hear them raging on in the distance. It was as though

177

someone had just turned off a switch and the bad weather over the gas station stopped.

I pushed myself up and stepped over to the window. Little bits of broken glass crunched underneath my shoes.

I could still see the lightning and hear the thunder, but it had moved past us. It hadn't been turned off, it was just done.

Nora stepped up next to me, standing so close her arm brushed against mine. I looked over at her and saw the barely noticeable smile she was wearing. My eyes followed her gaze to see what she was looking at.

The sun was pushing through the last gray storm cloud and stretching out across the sky was the brightest, boldest rainbow I'd ever seen. My hands were still shaking, but I was glad to see the storm leaving.

"Beautiful," Nora whispered, and I nodded. And it was, even though it seemed out of place in this dark, and dreary world we lived in. This wasn't a place for rainbows.

Looking out at the storm I couldn't help but wonder if it had been one of HOME's creations. As I watched it move away from the gas station, it seemed as though it was the same as any old storm I'd ever seen before. It had been a strong one, but it was just a regular storm… not one manufactured to reboot the Earth.

"Should we go?" I asked Nora even though I felt apprehensive. The sky was bright and clear to the north but the strange feeling in the air remained.

"Sure, let's grab the bags," she said walking

back towards the corner of the room we had been hiding in.

She picked up a few items scattered around the floor and put them back inside the bag before walking over to me. Nora handed me the bag I had packed. It still had the bottles of water inside.

I was tempted to open one and chug it down. Riding out the storm had made me thirsty.

"You found water?" Nora asked looking at me with a raised eyebrow.

"Yeah right before the storm came."

"Oh. I see."

"Let's go," I said carefully walking across the floor, trying to avoid any large shards of glass.

When I got to the window, I kicked at some of the glass before carefully stepping out of the opening. It would be easier than trying to pull open the squeaky, rusted door.

I watched Nora as she carefully made her way out of the window after me. She brushed herself off as she looked around.

"Which way?" Nora said while squinting at the horizon.

I looked up towards the sun pushing at the gray clouds. "This way," I said as I pointed to what I was pretty sure was the right direction. After having seen the map, I only felt a little more confident with my directions. Nora nodded and followed me down the street without question.

Many of the buildings in the area had broken windows, and the road was covered with deep puddles we tried to walk around. There were broken branches scattered all over the road,

179

showing the evidence of the storm that had roared through the area.

I wasn't sure how long we were inside of the gas station, but based on where the sun was in the sky, we had a good amount of daylight left. We'd be able to put in a couple miles if everything went well. I sighed thinking about how far from Penn and Carter we still were, but each mile would bring me that much closer.

All I could do was continue to hope they were still there waiting for me. Hopefully they hadn't gone out to try to find me. I wished I could tell them I was on my way. I didn't admit it to Nora, but I was weak, scared and in pain... I needed them. I needed Penn.

"What are you thinking about?" Nora said looking at me with her head tilted slightly to the side. I forced a small smile so she wouldn't see my sadness, although maybe she already had.

I looked away from her and shook my head, "Nothing. I just want to be there already."

"It must be really great... I never had anything I wanted to get back to. I mean, since the storms," she said, stepping around a large puddle.

I couldn't, nor did I want to, explain how important getting back to Penn and Carter was to me. It was all I wanted and all I'd keep fighting for. No matter where I was or whatever deterred me from getting to my destination, I would never give up trying to get back to Penn. And Carter too.

"We're probably going to have to camp outside again tonight," I said with a yawn. I didn't think we were going to have much luck finding somewhere to stay, and I was already tired. Sleeping outside never provided me enough rest, and with the injury I needed it even more.

"Yeah," Nora said looking up at the sky. The dark storm clouds were long gone. "Who knows, maybe we can find a house to stay in before it gets dark."

"Maybe, but let's put in as many miles as we possibly can. The sooner we get there, the better," I said knowing that probably didn't apply to her. She was likely nowhere near as excited to get there as I was.

She might be worried to meet new people. It wasn't like she knew them at all and she wouldn't have that same trust with them that I had. And really, she didn't even know me all that well. Nora was putting a lot of faith in me. It wasn't like she had a whole lot of choices, though. With things the way they were, no one had a lot of choices about anything.

"Yeah, of course," she said with a smile. "I'll go as fast as you want. Or can handle."

I nodded and moved my feet faster. Now that I knew how much we had to travel, it was easier to ignore the pain in my side just so I could get there. I wanted to push myself as hard as possible.

I wasn't sure how long or how far we had walked when the sun started to set. We hadn't stopped to eat, we just pulled snacks out of our bags and continued to move. There were times we slowed our pace, but we never stopped moving.

But now that we were losing daylight, we

181

were going to have to stop. Besides, rest would be good.

We walked another half of a mile or so, but never saw a single house. Even if we had, after what we'd been through, I probably wouldn't feel safe in it anyway.

"How about over there?" I said pointing to a small group of shrubs near a single tree with only half of its leaves remaining.

"Sure," Nora said, following me over to our campsite for the night. "Can we build a fire?"

"Can we, or should we? Do you even know how?" I asked narrowing my eyes at her.

She nodded slowly, "I do."

"Really?"

"Of course. Why would I lie about that?" she said digging in her bag and pulling out a lighter. "But I'm not sure if we should."

I looked around and while there were no houses, that didn't mean someone wouldn't come wandering this way, especially if they saw a fire. For all we knew, Marv was on his way.

Maybe he had gone back to his house and found his buddy lying there on the floor… murdered. And now he was out looking for whoever had done it. Maybe he'd seen us running away. There was always a chance we'd just happen to cross his path and he'd kill us for trespassing.

"I'm not sure it's a good idea," I said staring at the lighter. I wanted to feel the heat from a fire. My body craved the warmth, I needed it, but I also didn't want to be found. I was too close. To close to finding them.

182

"Yeah… OK," Nora said and I could tell she was disappointed, but understood. "I shouldn't have even asked. I know better than that. I just need to warm my bones."

"We can warm up when we get to my place," I said with a weak smile. I tried not to think about how Penn and Carter would receive Nora. Penn probably wouldn't be happy about it, but what choice did I have but to take her with me? I couldn't just abandon her, especially because she had the gun. It wouldn't be smart to be out here alone without a weapon.

I tried to find some dry leaves to sit on because the ground was still damp from the rain that had come through the area. The air was colder than it had been the night before, probably because of the storm. Nora's shivering indicated that she noticed it too.

Nora reached inside of her grocery bag and pulled out a granola bar. She took a bite and offered me the other half.

"No thanks," I said as my body shivered uncontrollably.

"You sure?"

"Yeah, I'm sure," I said holding up my palm.

Nora took a small bite, "I meant about the fire… we have a gun. It'll probably be OK. One of us stays awake while the other sleeps. Maybe just for a little while."

"I'm sure," I said feeling the doubts of my decision in my chilled bones. There was a part of me that wanted the fire and was willing to take the

183

risk, but then there was the other part of me that worried if we did, I'd never see Penn again. "No fire."

Nora shrugged, or maybe she just shivered, as she rolled damp leaves between her fingers. "Care if I sleep first?" she asked reaching behind her back for the gun.

"Nah, go ahead," I said taking the gun from her. She lowered herself to the ground and curled up into a tight ball.

"Thanks," she mumbled. Nora must have been tired from all the walking because within five minutes, I could tell by the rhythm of her breaths that she was sleeping.

I watched her as she slept. Her body started to jerk slightly and I knew she was dreaming. I watched as her hands and legs twitched while she made tiny whining noises.

My hand instinctively reached out to wake her, but when she grunted and turned slightly, I pulled back. She stretched her arm over her head and relaxed into what appeared to be a deeper sleep.

I was about to look away when something just under the collar of her shirt towards her shoulder caught my eye. It was so dark outside it was hard to make out what was there, but it appeared to be some kind of black marking.

I leaned in closer trying to angle myself so I didn't block out the dim light from the moon. For a second I moved away, feeling silly trying to look under the loosened fabric at her neck. It was probably a birthmark or a tattoo, but I couldn't help it. Curiosity got the better of me.

I moved in as close as I could, trying not to disturb her. And then I saw it. I knew exactly what I was looking at.

Chapter twenty.

It was a marking I had seen before, only on Nora it was on her shoulder. The tattoo was smaller, but it was just like the one Penn had.

I grabbed the gun tighter and stared at her sleeping, barely moving body with wide, unblinking eyes. After a slow, deep breath, I pointed the gun at her head.

It was the right thing to do. I had to do it. I should have known something wasn't right the second the facility put her into my room.

Was the facility part of HOME? Somehow it must have been connected. I couldn't think straight. I was confused. All I could think about was the HOME marking on Nora's shoulder. There was one thing I was pretty sure about and that was that Nora was a spy from HOME.

My teeth were pressed together so hard I started to worry they were going to break. I couldn't shoot someone in their sleep even if they were from HOME. Or could I?

I reached over and tried to lift the plastic grocery bag, but it crinkled and I was afraid the small noise would be enough to wake her. Even the damp leaves underneath me were too loud, but I had to get away… without the bag.

I moved in slow motion as I got to my feet.

186

My eyes were glued to her as I took small steps away. Each breath I took got stuck somewhere between my nose and my lungs. It was as though I had to think about each breath and push it out so I could take in fresh air.

After about ten steps, I turned around and started walking faster away from the campsite. I glanced back expecting to see her chasing me, but she wasn't. She was back on the ground behind the shrubs, sleeping peacefully.

My breathing quickened and panic set in. I was trying to get away from Nora, but I wasn't sure if I was walking in the right direction. Somehow I had gotten turned around and it felt as though I was walking in circles.

Even though it was cold, I started to sweat. I held out my arms keeping my palms out and my fingers spread so I could stop myself if I was about to walk into something.

Maybe it was just chance that she had been placed in my room at the facility, or maybe it had been intentional. I tried to think back to everything we had talked about. She had thought the facility was somehow linked to HOME… she had been the one to bring it up. But was it because she knew something? Testing me? Why?

How much of what she had told me was the truth and how much of it had been lies? Knowing that tattoo was on her, all I could do was assume everything that came out of her mouth had been a lie.

I was still walking, but my heart was beating as though I had been running a marathon.

187

When I heard the leaves crunching behind me, I knew it was her. And I knew she was moving fast.

I started to run without bothering to look over my shoulder. I only made it about ten steps before she flew into me knocking me down.

My face hit the ground and little grains of dirt went into my mouth. I tried to spit it out, but the gritty dirt was stuck in my teeth.

We were both grunting and breathing heavily as I rolled around to get away from her. The look on her face was frightening… and intimidating. The Nora looking at me wasn't the Nora I'd seen in the facility. This was a trained Nora.

"Ros! Stop it!" she said with a snort.

I tried to get the gun between us, but her hand was on top of mine, pushing the gun away. She grabbed my hand and tried to peel my fingers off of the handle.

I growled at her like an animal and held on as tightly as I could. The one thing I couldn't do was let go of that gun. Although it probably didn't matter that much, she could likely kill me with her bare hands if she wanted to. But the gun was my only chance to protect myself. Without it I'd have nothing at all.

"Argh! Stop it already!" she shouted at me with a snarl on her face. Little bits of spit flew out between her teeth. "Why are you doing this? After everything we've been through? I don't understand!"

I didn't answer.

"Why are you trying to leave me alone out

here?" she squealed.

She didn't know I had seen the tattoo. Nora simply thought I was abandoning her.

I didn't know what to say or even what I should do. There wasn't enough time to think of how to handle the situation before I heard the growls. Growls that didn't belong to me or Nora.

They were growls I'd heard before. I knew what was coming.

"Shit!" I hissed looking in the direction of the noises.

"Seriously! Why are you doing this? Why are you leaving me?" she asked with sadness and confusion filling her eyes.

"Shh!" I said aggressively as I peered into the darkness with Nora still on top of me. I couldn't see them... it was too dark, but I knew they were out there. Stalking us. "They're here."

She narrowed her eyes and shook her head, "What are you talking about? Who's here?"

"Shut up!" I ordered and Nora looked shocked, but listened. She stopped talking. I could tell by the look on her face that she finally had heard them too. "They're getting closer. We have to get out of here."

"Oh, now it's *we* is it?" she said looking down her nose at me.

"OK, stay here then, but get off of me," I said pushing at her shoulders.

She looked at me for a second as though she was weighing her options. I could feel her shoulders weaken and she rolled over and stood up. She looked down at me and stretched out her hand to help me up.

I took her hand. I couldn't look away from her eyes. There was a kindness in them, but I couldn't let myself fall for it. I knew the sort of things HOME was capable of. And Nora wasn't an exception.

"OK… now what?" Nora whispered looking into the darkness. The dog-beasts were still there. They weren't howling and grunting anymore but I could hear them breathing. They were close.

There was no doubt in my mind they were watching us… stalking us. And if one of them got me, I knew all too well what would happen afterward. I'd seen it before and there was no cure out here.

I started to walk backwards and Nora followed. She held out her hands on both sides as though she would use her arms as shields if she needed to. Didn't she know what the dogs would do to her?

Before I knew what was happening, I heard a rustle from a nearby bush. One of the dog-beasts leapt through the air towards me.

Time felt as though it had stopped long enough for me to get the gun up. I tried to point it at the dog just as time returned to normal speed. My fingers were clumsy, and I fumbled with the gun.

I twisted my body at the last second to move out of the way of the dog. Before I could even get the gun back into position, Nora had tackled the dog to the ground and was sitting on top of its back. Her legs were squeezed around its

190

middle so tight it squealed and squirmed.

Nora's hands moved so fast I couldn't even comprehend what she was doing until I heard the crunch from the bones in the dog's neck. She dropped the dog-beast's head, letting it flop hard to the ground.

Her hands had moved so quickly... it didn't seem like that had been the first time she had to break a dog-beast's neck. In fact, I'd go so far as to think she'd done it a lot.

She looked up at me and her expression was different... darker. It was as though there was a part of her that she had been hiding, but she couldn't hold it in any longer and she was worried I had noticed.

Perhaps it was all part of her HOME training, but now that her life was being threatened she wouldn't keep it hidden. It was like the same on switch Penn had, only he hadn't been able to turn his off.

Off to my right, I heard the growl of another dog-beast. I couldn't see it but somehow I knew it was coming for me.

Nora took several large steps towards me, grabbed my arm and spun me around. I looked down at my hands knowing something was different. I realized the gun was gone, and Nora was holding it.

She had it aimed directly at the dog-beast which slowed its approach. It was as though it knew what a gun was and what it would do to him.

The dog-beast started to retreat, but Nora didn't show mercy. Even though it might draw more attention, she pulled the trigger, hitting the dog in the forehead.

"Nice aim," I said unable to keep the sarcasm out of my voice.

She turned her body forty-five degrees and pointed the gun in my face. I lifted my hands up slightly, showing her my empty palms.

My heart was pounding so hard and fast I could feel it in the top of my head all the way down to my feet. "Please, Nora… don't."

"Why were you leaving me?" she said making a frown on one side of her mouth. It was like I was looking at two different people.

One Nora was sad and hurt, while the other was angry… quite angry. Possibly angry enough to actually pull the trigger if I didn't say the right things.

"I saw it," I said glancing down towards her shoulder.

"Saw what?" she asked pausing between the words.

I sneered at her, forgetting there was a gun pointed at my face, "The stupid HOME tattoo. I know what you are."

"And exactly what do you know about the tattoos, hmm?" she said tilting her head to the side.

"More than I'd like to," I said, but really I knew exactly as much as I needed to know. That those who had them were affiliated with HOME and not someone I wanted to be around.

"Oh, I see. Did it tell you that I escaped from HOME, barely with my life? Did it tell you how long ago I left them behind?" She lowered the gun for a second before pointing it at me again with a shaking hand, "Did the tattoo tell you what happened to my friends?"

"You told me they let you leave," I said narrowing my eyes.

Nora laughed, "You know so much about HOME, but you would actually believe they'd let someone go? They shot me when we ran," she said lifting up her shirt to show me what looked like a healed bullet wound on her side. "The only reason I'm alive today is because my friends saved me from that horrendous place... but I couldn't do the same for them. They didn't make it once we were out. Hell, I almost didn't either."

Nora looked sad and lowered the gun. I was pretty sure she wasn't going to kill me, but I would have felt more comfortable with the gun in my waistband.

In the distance a dog-beast let out a painful howl. It was like a war-cry. Perhaps the dog-beast was calling for backup.

"We should go," I said but Nora held out her palm to stop me.

"Are you just going to leave me out here again? I ran from HOME. I hate HOME. Please, please don't leave me out here alone. I've been through so much... just like you, I don't deserve to die out here after everything."

"Just like me?"

"Yeah, you've been out there before, trying to survive."

I shook my head, "I don't know what to say to you, Nora. HOME lies. HOME has spies

193

everywhere. You know that better than I do. I can't trust you."

"I've left that all behind. I'm not the first and I won't be the last. People try to escape them all the time," she said staring into my eyes.

I looked right back into hers. The dog-beasts were making it hard for me to concentrate.

"I haven't had any contact with HOME for months and months. Please, Ros, I have nowhere else to go. I have no one left. If you desert me, I'll die out here. You have to believe me," she said pulling on my sleeve.

There was another howl. It sounded closer.

I looked into Nora's eyes but I couldn't see anything. I couldn't tell if she was deceiving me, but what I did know was she hadn't tried to kill me. She'd killed the person at the facility and there were countless times she could have turned the gun on me and she hadn't. Instead she saved me... more than once.

Maybe she had left HOME behind. It was possible. Penn had done it.

"Urrrggg OK... OK, let's go. I won't leave you," I said moving my arms out in front of me so I wouldn't walk into anything.

"But, do you believe me?"

"Sure, OK, let's go." I lied. I didn't believe her. The only thing I could believe at this moment was that she wasn't going to kill me. At least not yet.

She nodded, but it didn't seem as though she was completely satisfied with my response. But she was going to accept it because round two of the dog-beasts were closing in on us. I didn't want to have round two and neither did she.

We couldn't afford to sit there and argue about whether or not I believed her. We had to move. And that's exactly what we did.

We ran.

Chapter twenty-one.

We ran until we couldn't hear the dog-beast anymore. Nora held out her arm so that I'd stop.

I leaned forward slightly, trying to catch my breath while she closed her eyes and tried to focus on what she could, or couldn't, hear. It didn't seem like they were following us any longer. I was pretty sure they had given up, but I waited to see if Nora would concur.

After a minute her eyes popped open. She breathed heavily while she stared at me. My body shook when she broke the silence.

"I don't hear them. They must have stopped."

I nodded.

"Guess we won't be getting much sleep tonight," she said as she spun in a small circle looking at our surroundings.

"Guess not. Ugh," I said trying to figure out which direction we were facing. I hit my fist into my thigh repeatedly. I couldn't contain my frustration.

"What is it?"

"I don't know if we were running the right way… in fact I don't think we were," I said feeling like I was all turned around. That wasn't the only part of my frustrations though. I was also frustrated I hadn't realized she was from HOME, and even more frustrated that I didn't know what to do about it.

It felt as though I didn't have a choice. I was stuck with her. I didn't know how to get away.

Nora put her hand on her hip and looked around. "Hmm."

"I think that way," I said pointing towards my left, but I was just guessing. I wouldn't know until the sun came over the horizon. "We have to wait for morning."

I didn't want to keep traveling. If we walked in the wrong direction, we could inadvertently be putting extra miles between us and our final destination. That was something I didn't want to do. Maybe we already had.

After what had happened with the dog-beasts, I knew we couldn't stay in the wide open. At least I didn't feel as though we could.

"Let's walk a little... see if we can find a place to stop for a bit?" I said, but it sounded more as though I was asking for her permission.

"Sure," Nora said looking up at the sky and then pointing off to the left. I shrugged but walked with her. For all I knew, finding directions had been part of her training.

We walked in silence. All I could hear were the random howls from the distant dog-beasts and tiny chirps from the occasional cricket.

"I think that place, the facility we were in, was HOME," Nora said without turning to look at me. She turned her head slightly side to side as she scanned the horizon.

"Yeah, you thought that when we were

there, didn't you?"

"I did… my guess is that their purpose was to brainwash us into going back to HOME. You said you'd been there before, right?"

"Yeah," I said with a shaky voice. I couldn't remember exactly how much I told her, but it hadn't been much. Had I said I'd been there? Dammit!

Nora twisted at one of her fingers, "But why would they even want us back? Especially me. I'm not sure how you got away from them, but when me and my friends escaped, I killed a few of them."

"I'm not sure," I said with a small shrug. Why would HOME want either of us back? If that was their facility they could have just killed me. Why would they want anyone back that escaped from them? It wasn't like they could trust us.

I was so tired that I knew I wouldn't be able to make sense of any of it. Maybe it didn't even make sense.

The only thing I knew for sure was that I couldn't take Nora back to our place. If there was even a small chance she was still affiliated with HOME, I couldn't take the risk. And there was no way I could ever know for sure if she was still with HOME or not.

"Why did you leave HOME?" I asked, my voice soft.

"I hated it there! It was… I don't know, like being trapped with zombies," Nora said turning to look at me. Her eyes were wide and pleading as though she was begging me to believe her. "I just

198

didn't like how I felt there… it was like something just wasn't right. I didn't want to be part of it. So, we decided to leave."

Her words reminded me of how I had felt about HOME. I never liked HOME even when I didn't have any solid evidence for not liking them. Now that I had evidence, well I hated them even more.

They'd taken Ryan, transformed him into something he wasn't and had him working in their army. I'd seen them shoot down one of their own during our escape. And even though I'd forgiven Penn, I still remembered what he'd done for HOME.

If they could do all that and more, maybe they would be able to convince people like Nora and me to team up with them. They probably had their methods.

"What happened to your friends?"

Nora looked down at her feet and then turned her face away so I couldn't see her. "One got sick… he died. The other was bit by one of those demon dogs." There was a long pause before she turned to face me with tears streaming down her face. "I had to kill him."

I could feel my face mirroring her sadness. The memory of Seth burning himself alive played through my mind. I had to fight away the images of Sienna as she got sicker and sicker. I didn't want to think about it because then I would think of Dean… and the barn. If I thought about that it could paralyze me, and I had to get back to what I had left.

199

"Sorry," I said wishing I wouldn't have asked. I knew they hadn't made it, I should have just left it at that.

"Yeah, I'm sure we've all lost someone," she said looking at me again, and I nodded as I fought back my tears.

We walked in silence for several minutes before a broken-down shack came into view. I swallowed down the gross taste in my mouth and pointed.

The decrepit building wouldn't provide much shelter, but it would hide us for long enough to get some rest. I couldn't even guess how many hours of night we had left, but it couldn't be many. Soon the sun would rise and give a little light to our dark and dreary world.

We stepped inside the small shack. It was just one large empty room the size of a small bedroom with a single small window near the door. There wasn't a bathroom, kitchen or furniture… nothing. It was completely empty.

The wooden walls looked swollen as though they'd been retaining water. The flooring had been torn out, and we were walking on packed down dirt.

"Weird place," Nora whispered as though she thought someone might hear and would be offended.

"Wonder what it was used for," I said but Nora just shrugged as she closed the door.

The room was cold, but at least it was somewhere to hide out while we rested. It was far better than being stuck out there with whatever was waiting for us.

I sat down in the dirt and hugged my sides. Nora stepped up to the crooked window and stared outside.

"Sleep, I'll watch," she said clasping her hands behind her back.

I reluctantly leaned my head back. No matter how much it seemed as though she'd been through a similar experience to mine, I still couldn't bring myself to trust her. It was probably all part of her training.

There probably wasn't any way I could actually believe that she had left HOME. Even if she had left, she had worked with them closely enough that she'd allowed them to put their marking on her skin. But what did her tattoo mean? What was her position with HOME? How long had she worked for them before she supposedly escaped?

Even though I couldn't trust anything she said, I didn't feel like I had many choices considering she was the one holding the gun. Winter would be here before I knew it and I didn't know how long until the snow would start to fall. I had to get back to Penn and Carter before it did. I didn't want to die out here.

Nora would just have to come with me unless I could figure out how to get away from her. Of course, that was probably pretty unlikely now that I'd been caught attempting it once already.

She was still trained by HOME. I had to be careful. I'm wasn't sure there was anything I could do. I felt helpless. It was like I was being held hostage, but I was the one bringing her to my own place.

When I woke up, Nora was leaning her arm on the windowsill, her eyes taking long blinks. She was exhausted. It was kind of amazing she hadn't fallen asleep.

"Rest," I said pushing myself up off of the ground. My side was still stiff and sore, but I didn't think it would improve until I was back with Penn and Carter, safe and sound. Then I'd be able to rest and heal. "I'll watch for a bit. Go on, get some sleep."

"You sure? I know you want to keep moving…."

"We'll move quicker after you've had some rest," I said, and she nodded. I got up and looked out the window. The morning sky was a shade of blue and everything was still, it felt peaceful.

She stared at the ground for several minutes before she lowered herself down onto the same spot I had been laying, and curled herself into a small ball. I couldn't take my eyes off of the gun poking out of the back of her waistband.

I wasn't the least bit surprised she hadn't offered it to me. If I would have asked for it, I knew she wouldn't have given it.

I considered sneaking out of the little shack, but I was pretty sure that if I tried the squeaking door would wake her. She'd have the gun against my skull in a matter of seconds. Or maybe she'd even shoot, although it really seemed like she didn't want to be left alone.

I didn't risk it. I still had time to come up with a plan… *if* I could come up with a plan.

After she rested for what felt like several hours, I decided to wake her. My anxiety of not moving was getting the better of me.

We walked the rest of the day continuing to head north. I found various edibles along the way but nothing that satisfied our hunger. I'd even found a small stream that we had been able to drink from. We couldn't boil the water, so we had to risk it.

My stomach growled for more, but the leaves were better than having nothing at all. "You must be used to not eating very often, huh?"

"What?" Nora said scrunching her nose up at me. "What do you mean?"

"You came into the facility starving to death… I just assumed you must have been used to not having much to eat."

"Oh, yeah, I guess so… I mean, I don't think you ever get used to it, do you?" She looked as though she was having a hard time moving her feet. She didn't have the same motivation that I had. I wanted to get back to Penn and Carter, but she didn't know what she was walking into.

We were both hungry and tired, but I had something driving me that she didn't. Friends. And hopefully they were still there waiting for me.

Chapter twenty-two.

We walked the rest of the day without anything slowing us down. Nothing around us was familiar, but I didn't let myself think about how much further we had left to go. Instead, I just let myself be happy for the good time we'd been making so far. Even our hunger wasn't stopping us. I was determined.

I couldn't guess how far the facility was from my home with Penn and Carter, but I knew they had taken me by car to get to there. When I saw the map at the gas station, I knew it would take longer than I would have liked to reach our destination.

What I was surprised about was the lack of homes and cities along the path we were making to get there. We didn't follow the roads as much as we should have, instead we just tried to walk a straight line whenever possible.

We walked through small wooded areas and open fields. The lack of homes probably had something to do with the storms that had gone through when our lives had been erased to a clean slate. It was likely that the copious amounts of tornadoes had come through Michigan and ripped homes right off of their foundation just as they had in other states.

Some places seemed to have been hit harder

than others. At least that's what I'd seen in my travels and based on what I was seeing, I would guess that Michigan had been hit hard. I just hoped we'd find somewhere to stay at night, because after our run in with the dog-beasts, I didn't like the idea of camping outside.

Nora and I didn't talk much as we made our way across the land. Thankfully, things had been rather uneventful, and even though there was still daylight left, when I saw the small shed that looked like it was being held up by a couple slim birch trees, I suggested we just stop for the night.

"Hmm… are you sure?" Nora said looking towards the sky. "We could probably squeeze in another hour or two of walking."

"I know, but what I don't know is if we'll find somewhere to stop," I said walking towards the shed without waiting for her to agree.

When we got closer, I saw the door was still attached, but it was far from secure. I lightly touched it and it squeaked as it swayed back and forth.

"Sure about this?" Nora asked looking around the area as though she thought she might just happen to find something better. But of course, there wasn't anything as far as the eye could see.

I stepped inside the dirt covered shed that was no bigger than an average bathroom. The only thing inside was a grime covered lawn mower.

"I'm sure," I said closing the door as best as I could once she was inside. The shed was far from warm, but it was better than being out in the open. Cool air leaked in through the poorly fitting door and the window opposite the door that had a wide crack running from top to bottom.

Even though we could only see out in one direction, I was pretty sure we would be able to hear someone coming through the thin walls. The nights were so quiet it seemed as though we could hear for miles and miles.

The day couldn't have passed by any better than it had. We'd made good progress. The only thing that could have been better was finding more food.

Thanks to Carter, I knew how to find some things, although it wasn't enough to keep either of us feeling satisfied. But it was enough to keep us alive for another day.

Nora sat down on the ground and wrapped her arms around her body. It looked as though she was trying to make herself as small as possible.

"Ehhh!" she squealed as she shook her body violently and then popped up to her feet.

"What's going on?" I said bending my knees slightly as I faced the door. I put my hands out as though I was ready to fight.

"Beetle!" she said flapping her hands all over her clothing as she flicked away invisible bugs. "A big, gross, black beetle." She shivered and closed her eyes as she stood up on her toes.

"Where?"

She shook her head, "I don't know, I lost it! It ran across my foot and... I... I lost sight of it!"

The girl from HOME was afraid of bugs. I was slightly surprised she hadn't pulled out her gun and killed the bug after it dared to climb on her.

Her hands shook as she flicked at dirty bits of lint on her clothing.

I watched as her body trembled. I wasn't sure if she was shaking because she was cold or because she was thinking about the bug that had just crawled across her shoe. She pointed at the ground about five feet away from her, "There! Look at it!"

After my heart popped back into a calmer rhythm, I tilted my head and looked down at the bug. It was bigger than I had imagined.

"Eww, that is gross," I said kicking at it gently with the tip of my shoe. I was trying to show it the way out, as if it would understand.

"Kill it," she said with wide eyes.

I raised an eyebrow at her, "You kill it."

"Umm, no... I hate bugs. I really, really, really hate bugs. Especially big bugs. Like beetles. There are probably hundreds of them in here," she said as her eyes darted around the walls as if she was already seeing them climbing down the walls looking for her.

The corner of my mouth curled up slightly, "If there were hundreds of those bugs in here, trust me, you'd know it."

"Oh. OK. That makes me feel so much better," Nora said taking a step backwards. When her back lightly brushed up against the wall, she jumped forwards as though she'd just been tapped on the shoulder by another beetle. "I can't stay in here."

"Yes you can," I said shaking my head.

"No, I don't think I can."

I considered talking about the bugs nonstop. If I made it seem like it was worse than it actually was, maybe she'd leave. But if I did trick her into leaving, she'd still have the gun, and there wouldn't be anything to stop her from just waiting outside until morning.

"There are no more bugs in here than there are out there," I said tilting my head towards the window.

"Again, that makes me feel so much better," she pressed her hands into her forehead and groaned. "OK, OK... I can do this. Where is it now?"

I looked around at the floor and shrugged. "It probably left."

"No, he's there," she said pointing where the wall touched the ground.

Nora took a deep breath and scoured the ground before she sat back down in the middle of the floor. Her eyes were glued to the big, black beetle that was making its way towards the door. Maybe he didn't want to be trapped in here with her either.

"Why don't you get some sleep first," I said leaning against the wall by the window. "You didn't get much last night."

"Neither did you."

"But you got even less."

"Hmm," she said not looking away from the beetle. "I guess I should."

She turned around and studied the wall before she scooted and leaned back against it. There was no way she was going to lay down in the

208

dirt with a chance a bug might crawl on her while she slept. Sitting on the floor and leaning against the wall was bad enough.

How had she even survived out in the wilderness? Although it had seemed as though there were fewer bugs, but maybe she hadn't spent a lot of time outdoors. Maybe whatever her job with HOME was didn't require a lot of outdoor missions.

"If it comes back... keep it away from me, OK?" Nora asked between half-closed eyes.

"I will."

For my shift, I spent most of the time watching out the window trying not to fall asleep. I was beyond tired, but my ears and eyes were what would potentially keep us alive. What I was feeling was probably similar to what Penn had felt any time he had to keep watch over us.

The night passed by slowly. We alternated our turns, but they were short. Once one of us fell asleep, we didn't stay asleep for long. Some rest was probably better than no rest.

The short bursts of sleep made me feel even more tired, but once I woke, it was hard to fall back asleep. My mind would just start going with worries and anxieties. Nora must have felt the same way because her sleep was following a similar pattern.

The second I saw the blackness in the window turn into a brighter, pale blue color, I knew the sun was starting to come up. I looked at Nora who was pushing herself up off of the ground.

"Morning?" she said squinting at the still

mostly dark window.

I was about to answer when I saw movement out of the corner of my eye. My eyes shifted, and I covered my mouth when I saw the shadowy figure moving across the grass.

Nora noticed my reaction. "What is it?" she asked.

I violently waved my hands, begging her to stop talking with my eyes. Nora's eyes narrowed, and she came up next to me. She cautiously peeked out of the window.

I pushed her back so she was out of the way. If she wasn't careful the person out there might catch her looking. Or maybe he would be able to hear the faint noises of her body movements.

I knew when I met her eyes she had seen him. She was just as freaked out to see the stranger as I was.

She grabbed my arm as I started to move back towards the window. I shrugged her off and looked out just in time to see him walk out of view.

"Is he gone?" Nora mouthed almost silently.

I shook my head. Just because I didn't see him, didn't mean he wasn't still there.

Chapter twenty-three.

Both Nora and I looked at the flimsy door which might as well have been miles away from us. If the person outside wanted to come in, there wouldn't be anything to stop him except for a bullet from Nora's gun.

I caught her eyes and shifted mine down towards her waistband. She nodded, but her eyes were wide and glossy. Nora looked just as frightened as I felt.

Her hands shook as she pointed the gun at the door. I slowed my breathing and turned back towards the window.

I had no idea where he had gone. Maybe he had just been passing through. I couldn't see him, but that didn't mean he had left. It was possible he already knew we were here, and he was waiting for us to step out and into his trap. Or maybe we already were in his trap.

I couldn't talk to Nora. There were so many holes and cracks in the shed that if we spoke, we'd risk being found. Maybe the guy wouldn't even care. Hopefully, he was just passing through, but it was better to be safe than sorry.

The second I saw him come back into view I stared at Nora to get her attention, but her eyes were glued to him. I tapped her forearm, and she turned her head sharply. Her eyes were wide and

211

her mouth hung open as though she was struggling to take in air.

The man was wearing a knit hat pulled down to just above his eyes. With his head down, I couldn't see his face.

He kept turning his head over his shoulder as he walked back in the other direction. Then I saw what he was looking at. I wanted to scream. I wanted to run. My stomach threatened to send out everything that was inside of it.

The guy yanked on a rope which was attached to the neck of another man. The slim body bounced hard against the ground while it colored the dying grasses blood red.

"Oh shit," Nora said almost soundlessly. Her voice was like a gentle breeze passing by my ear.

We both watched in horror as he dragged the body until we couldn't see either of them anymore. The man could have been just out of our view, or he could have kept walking further away. We had no way of knowing where he was or where he was going. All I knew was that we had to get out of the shed before he was staining the ground with our blood.

"What should we do?" she said with a shallow breath.

I shook my head and stared at the door. My whole body was shaking. If the man opened the door, and Nora wasn't fast enough with her shot, it would be the end for us. And based on what I'd seen outside the window, it didn't look like it would be a pleasant ending.

"We have to run for it," Nora whispered as she peered out of the window, trying to see as far as she could.

She was probably right. Maybe the man was gone. But maybe he'd come back, and now was our only chance.

Nora put her hands on my shoulders and looked into my eyes. I could feel the coldness of her hands through my clothing. Her lip vibrated as her body shivered, "Open the door, step to the side and I'll get ready to shoot. If he's not there, run. Just run as fast as you can and I'll follow."

I moved my head up and down slowly as though I was afraid if I moved it fast it would make too much noise. Were we doing the right thing? All I knew was that I wanted to get away as soon as we possibly could.

"On three," she whispered. She waited until I was standing by the door to raise her fingers. After a deep breath, she lowered them one by one and when she finished, I opened the door.

The look of relief that washed down her face let me know he wasn't there. I carefully looked out of the door and gestured for her to follow.

We turned out the door in the opposite direction the man had gone and started to run. Before I could stop, the man stepped out from the side of the shed and I slammed into his solid body.

I could hear the scream inside of me before it burst out of my lungs and into his chest. I backed away almost tripping over myself as I tried to escape.

213

He looked at me with his dark eyes. His lips curled up before he let out a laugh that chilled my bones.

Nora pulled my shirt and dragged me away from the man. I saw her point the gun at him, but it bounced up and down with each step she took. She looked as though she was having trouble lining up her shot.

"Shoot him!" I hollered, but she turned us around the other side of the shed. He disappeared from view but I could still hear him laughing. "Why aren't you killing him?"

I kept looking behind us to see if I could catch a glimpse, but I couldn't find him. He wasn't there. Nora abruptly let go of me and it felt as though I was falling through the earth. I tried to regain my balance but miscalculated and stumbled backward. What felt like a branch hooked around my ankle, I was too tangled up to save myself from heading straight for the ground.

I stretched out my arms in an attempt to stop myself from hitting too hard. It was like I was moving in slow motion as I fell to the ground. My body landed much softer than I thought it would... somehow I must have managed to soften the blow.

I blinked to clear my vision. I looked at the ground around me, only it wasn't the ground I had landed on. Staring back at me was a man with a blood streaked face and a rope tied tightly around his neck. He didn't move.

His eyes were wide as he gawked at me. It seemed as though he was looking right through me. He blinked his eyes and then coughed, his voice was rough, "Please kill me."

I scrambled backwards trying to get away from him. I wasn't sure if he was actually alive or if I was only imagining what was happening. Nora reached out her hand to me and I quickly took it.

"Kill me!" the bloody man begged in a raspy voice. A small stream of blood oozed out of the corner of his mouth when he pressed his lips together. He gurgled and started to choke before coughing out a splattering of blood droplets.

I turned around looking for the man that was responsible. "Where is he?" I squeaked.

If we didn't get away, we'd soon be laying down on the muddy ground next to the blood splattered man. Unless Nora could land a shot.

"Where did he go, Nora?" I asked again.

"I don't know," she said and let go of my hand. She took a few steps back and waved me along, "Come on."

She started to run, and I didn't hesitate to follow. My feet couldn't move as fast as I wanted them to. Every step felt like I was trying to walk a straight line while being spun on a merry-go-round.

When I heard the crack of a gun, I put my hands over my head and screamed. I could hear him laughing in the distance and then another shot rang out. He wasn't messing around.

"Shoot back!" I shouted at Nora. I looked at her for only a second, afraid of taking my eyes off of the ground in front of me for too long. The last thing I wanted was to trip and fall while being shot at.

Nora looked over her shoulder and raised up

the gun. She was trying to aim, but she seemed frustrated.

"Just shoot," I said. It was like she was trying to get the perfect shot, but any shot would do.

Finally, when it seemed like she wasn't going to shoot, she pulled the trigger. The pop of the gun was louder than I had expected and my body jolted.

The man cried out, and I turned around hoping I'd see him falling to the ground. But all I saw was blood dripping down from his hand. The accuracy I'd seen from Nora wasn't there.

"Bitch!" he shouted in a deep voice that echoed through the trees.

"Got him," she said, but she knew she hadn't landed a shot that would stop his pursuit.

The man shot at us again, and again, and again. He was pulling the trigger carelessly. I couldn't tell if he was angrier about having been shot or that we were getting away.

After a pause, he shot again. This one sounded further away. We were putting distance between us and him. He was still trying to shoot us, but he had stopped chasing. He knew he couldn't catch us.

"SHIT!" he shouted again with a voice so loud it seemed to rumble through the earth. I turned around to see if I could spot him, but I couldn't. We had lost him. At least for now.

"What the hell was that about?" Nora said pulling at my arm. "What was he doing?"

I swallowed hard. "I... I have no idea!"

"We have to keep moving," Nora said looking at me.

And that was what we did. We kept moving. All day and even into the night, we didn't stop. We kept moving even in the darkness.

It was slow going, and we had to be careful not to lose our way, but we managed. And even when we got so tired we thought we couldn't go any further, the fear of being followed powered us to keep going.

We had been walking for so long my feet couldn't do it anymore. No matter how much my mind wanted to keep going, my feet needed to rest.

I had blisters on my toes and heels, some of which had popped and felt as though they were on fire. When Nora took off her shoes, I saw she was suffering from much of the same.

After all the walking we had done, we agreed to stop for a few hours. We'd found an abandoned house and locked ourselves in a second story bedroom. I didn't feel safe, but I couldn't remember the last time I had.

Things were bad. Nora hadn't stopped shaking since leaving the shed. Her skin was pale, and she had dark circles under her eyes. We hadn't eaten anything substantial in so long, that I knew without asking that she was in desperate need of food.

I was hungry too, but for some reason I was coping much better. This wasn't the first time I'd went without food for this long. I'd been doing all right managing with what water and food we did find along the way since leaving our bags of food

217

behind. All we had to do was make it to my home, and we'd have food. Lots of food.

My feet were so sore that now that I had my shoes off, I didn't know if I'd ever be able to get them back on again. I aggressively massaged my swollen feet, hoping to make them feel better so I could get my shoes back on. If something happened, I'd need to be ready.

When we weren't moving, the pain in my side screamed at me. It seemed as though it was getting worse. Even worse than what it had been when we left the facility.

We were in rough shape. The thought that we might not make it actually crossed my mind.

Nora laid down on the floor and curled herself up into a tight ball. She stared at the wall with her eyes wide open. She clutched the gun in her hand.

"I'll go downstairs and look for something," I said trying to stand on my bare feet. I hit my socks against my thigh trying to get as much dirt out of them as possible.

"No!" she said tilting her head up. "Don't leave me! Please don't leave me up here alone!"

I carefully lowered myself down, "You need to eat something."

"I will… we'll go together. Just… just let me rest a little first. I'm so tired," she said, but she didn't close her eyes. She put her head back down and stared at the wall.

"OK, when you're ready… but not too long. I'm hungry too," I said twisting my body awkwardly so I could rub my ankles without pulling the muscles in my side.

She took a slow breath and let it out of her nose loudly, "Thank you."

After twenty minutes or so, she fell asleep. I considered taking the gun from her just in case someone came and I needed it, but I was afraid if I tried to take it, it would wake her. She would sense someone was there and she'd pull the trigger. She wouldn't even bother to look. Plus, there was always the problem that if she caught me trying to disarm her she might shoot me on purpose.

We had probably only been resting for a few hours before my anxiety got the better of me. "We should get moving. Let's check for food and go."

"What? No! It'll be night in a few hours... we should just wait until morning," Nora said, half-heartedly crossing her arms. She was still weak, which was plainly obvious, but I didn't think she'd ever really admit how bad thing were for her.

"I think maybe we're close. The sooner we get there the better, and the safer we'll both be. If we put in a few more hours, maybe we can make it there by the end of the day."

I didn't know if it was my brain or my desire to get back to Penn and Carter that was driving me. It just seemed to me, even though nothing seemed familiar, we had to be close. We'd walked for days... I just wanted to see Penn again. I just wanted to feel a little safer.

Nora looked at me for a long moment and let out a long sigh. She must have been able to tell that I already had my mind made up.

"Fine. How close do you think we are? A

mile? Less? More?"

"Probably more… I'm not sure," I said as I tightened my laces. My shoes felt slightly damp, and the material rubbed annoyingly against my blisters.

Nora winced as she stood. She sniffed as she gestured with the gun for me to lead the way. I rolled my eyes and shook my head, but opened the door. Since she was the one with the gun, she should have led… or at the very least, she should have given me the gun.

We checked the kitchen, but it was mostly empty. I imagined someone had raided the house a long time ago. We made our way out of the house and walked north as the sun lowered itself down towards the horizon.

"This is a bad idea," Nora mumbled.

"Staying in one place isn't great either," I said raising my eyebrow.

I didn't think we walked even two full hours before the sun was starting to set. At least the clouds weren't out, and we would have some moonlight to help show the way.

The days were getting shorter, and colder. Our time was running out. It was almost as if I could actually hear it ticking in the silence. Even though moving was hard, we forced ourselves forward.

With each step, I started to doubt myself. I didn't know what I was doing. What if I had been leading us in the wrong direction all this time? What if I had been wrong about where our house was?

I glanced down at my feet as they moved across the dead grass and leaves. What if I was doing the wrong thing? We shouldn't have left the house. We should have waited until morning. Maybe we should go back and lock ourselves up. Take a day to regroup. We weren't that far from the house… we could go back.

I looked up to ask Nora if she thought we should go back but she wasn't there. She was gone, and I was all alone.

Chapter twenty-four.

"Nora!" I screamed as I took a step forward. The world looked as though it was being pulled away as I started falling towards the center of the Earth.

I reached out my hands trying to grab on to anything to stop my fall, but I couldn't. My fingertips scraped against something rough, but there was nothing to hold on to.

I hit the ground with a hard thud. Everything was quiet. All I could hear was my heavy, frantic breathing.

And then it rushed through my body like a tidal wave. My eyes pinched shut as I grabbed at my side and I howled at the pain rippling through my body.

When I opened my eyes, something was scurrying towards me. I tried to scream, but a hand clamped down over my mouth.

"Shh!" Nora said, her wide eyes glowing in the darkness. She aggressively tapped her finger against her lips.

I looked up and could see the darkening blue-gray sky between the tree branches. We were in a deep, grave-like hole, nearly encapsulated with dirt, and it felt like it was closing in on us.

"We have to get out of here," I said feeling dreadfully claustrophobic.

"No shit," Nora said looking around as though she was trying to find a secret staircase.

She watched me carefully as she stepped away. It almost looked as though she was afraid of what I might do. Nora pushed her hands against the mud wall surrounding us.

I tried to muffle my grunts as I stood up. My lungs tightened and I coughed when I tried to straighten my spine. The movements sent needles prickling into my side.

Nora glared at me and I knew she was annoyed I wasn't being completely silent. I waved my hand at her and curled myself at the waist.

She kicked her foot into the mud and little bits of dirt rained down on her from above. Nora turned and smiled at me as she stuck her foot in a little deeper. I watched her as she pushed herself up higher.

She kicked another hole into the mud, but this one didn't seem like it was going to work. The confidence disappeared from her face as the dirt crumbled out from under her foot. Nora could tell it wasn't going to support her weight much longer. She tried to shift her weight quickly so she would be supported by the last hole, but it too crumbled, causing her to crash down to the ground.

Nora landed on her bottom and looked up as the dirt from above rained down onto her hair. She let out a big sigh and hit her thighs with tight fists.

"OK," she said turning to look at me in the darkness. The whites of her eyes glowed. "Give me a boost."

"What?" I said looking up at the rectangular

opening trying to judge the height.

She followed my gaze and then looked back at me, "Give me a boost. I think maybe I can reach the top. I can get out... go find help."

"Who are you going to find that will come help me?" I said in a soft, yet squeaky voice. "You're just going to leave me down here to die! How about *you* give me a boost?"

"I can't."

"And why not?" I scowled at her.

She looked down at my side, "Try lifting your arms over your head."

Nora was right. I probably couldn't do it. Not to mention she probably wouldn't give me the gun even if I could get to the top.

Maybe I was overly paranoid about Nora, but really, who would she find to help me? Even if she could find someone, would she even be able to find her way back to me? I'd be stuck in this hole until whoever dug it came back to check their traps.

"I won't leave you. I promise. I'll find your friends. Give me the directions. What am I looking for?"

"How about you try to give me a boost and I'll go get help?" I said through pursed lips. "We could at least try."

She shook her head, "Can you even stand up without crouching over? How are you going to pull yourself up? You're not thinking clearly."

I swallowed hard knowing I couldn't. She was right and I didn't want to admit it. I didn't have any choice but to try to help her up. Either we both die down here in the pit, or I take my chances and help her out.

"Tell me about your friends... what are their names?" she said rubbing her hands together.

I sighed, "Penn and Carter."

"And I know I have to go north, but what am I looking for? How will I know it's your place when I see it?"

I described the house in as much detail as I could remember. "But when you find them... be very careful."

Nora tilted her head, "Why?"

"They aren't going to be expecting you. They will be protective," I said warning her with both my tone and my eyes.

She nodded as if she understood. "I'll figure something out."

"Please don't leave me down here," I said, looking away when my eyes started to fill with tears.

"I will come back. I promised you that I would," she said and looked back up towards the top of the pit. "Bend your knees and brace yourself."

My legs were already bent. She helped me over to the corner of the pit and stepped on my knee like it was the first rung of a ladder.

Nora pulled herself up, digging her hands into the mud. She slowly shifted her weight onto my back as she reached up higher into the wall. Dirt crumbled down and into my hair as she stepped onto my shoulders.

"Stand taller," she demanded.

"I can't."

"You have to try! I'm so close!"

I growled and forced myself to straighten. She was holding herself up with the wall, but still it was a lot of weight on my weak body and injured ribs.

When she started to slip, I reached up with my good arm and steadied her foot, and forced myself to stand as upright as I could manage.

"I got it," she said, and I felt her weight leave my body. I looked up and saw her throw her elbow over the edge. She grunted as she pulled herself up and out of the pit.

I smiled for a second but then she looked down at me and the smile vanished. She didn't say anything before she quickly turned her head as though she'd heard a noise and then I didn't see her anymore. She was gone.

"Nora!" I whispered, but of course she didn't respond. I pushed myself hard against the corner of the pit trying to make myself invisible. If there was someone up there, I didn't want them to find me. I had to try to survive as long as possible in case Nora did actually find me help.

I wasn't sure how I would survive at the bottom of the pit without food or water. Nora and I had already been surviving on so little that I didn't think I had much time left. All I could do was hope she'd find Penn and Carter, and then somehow they'd find me practically buried underground.

I looked up at the top of the pit. It seemed so far away… almost as though the walls were growing as I stared at the edges.

I tried to lift my arm over my head but the

pain limited my reach. "Oww… dammit," I said pushing my hand against my face.

I had to try something. I couldn't just sit here and wait for Nora to return. For all I knew she just ran away and wouldn't even bother trying to get me help. Would I have tried to find help for her? I shook my head as if to erase the question, because I didn't want to know the answer.

She probably was already on her way back to the facility or the nearest HOME location. Maybe she was on one of those communication devices calling for help, but not the kind of help that I wanted.

The mud around me was damp to the touch. I dug my fingers into it about a foot off of the ground. I could feel the bits of dirt and grime sneaking under my fingernails as I pressed my hand deeper.

If I could dig my foot holes deep enough, maybe I could climb my way out. I didn't know if my body would cooperate, but I had to try. If I was careful and took my time, maybe it would work.

It was difficult to dig into the hard, damp, rocky dirt, but I kept working. I stuck my foot into the first hole after I finished and pushed myself up just to see if it would hold me.

Even though I was approximately a foot closer to the top, it didn't feel like I had moved at all. I lowered myself back down and started working on the next hole.

When I finished the second, I stepped into the first hole as I dug my fingertips into the dirt. I pressed my body tight to the wall and slid my other foot into the second hole. I slowly shifted my weight.

The sides of my mouth curled into an impish smile. It seemed as though it was working.

But before I could get too excited, I felt my foothold weakening underneath me. The smile quickly dropped from my face. Just like Nora, I lost my confidence. I wasn't even sure I'd be able to make it to the top without using more arm strength. Arm strength I didn't have.

I looked up to judge how much further I had to go, but had to close my eyes when bits of dirt rained down into them. My hand automatically reached up to try to brush the grains out of my eyes. When I let go of the wall with my good hand, my left foot hole collapsed underneath me and I dropped down to the ground.

"Shit!" I said grabbing a handful of dirt and throwing it against the wall opposite me. I balled up my hands and slammed them into the mud floor.

I looked up at the quickly darkening sky. Even though I wanted to scream into the darkness that felt as though it was drowning me, I didn't. I was too afraid of what might be up there... of who might find me alone, trapped in this pit.

This was my personal hell for everything I had done.

Tears streamed down my face and I didn't even bother trying to stop them. The wetness mixed with the dirt, making my cheeks feel tight.

I wiped at the tears as the world around me turned black. I was really all alone. The only thing I had was my thoughts... stuck in what I assumed would be my grave.

I curled up into a ball and sobbed until there was nothing left.

Chapter twenty-five.

It was hard for me to keep count but I was pretty sure it had been two days since Nora deserted me. Most of the time I just lay there stuck in an almost dreamlike state. Or I was actually sleeping.

I was weak.

I wasn't going to survive.

No food.

No water.

Nothing.

Just me and my thoughts.

I popped up onto my knees and started clawing into the mud-packed floor. If I could dig a hole deep enough, maybe I could get water.

I scratched and dug into the dirt, making a hole at least six inches deep, but nothing oozed through the mud. I picked up a handful of dirt from the bottom of my little hole and squeezed it in my fist. My hand cramped up before I could even force out half of a drop.

"Ahhhh!" I said in a raspy, weak voice. I tried to shout, but my voice barely existed.

It didn't matter who heard me. All I wanted was to get out of this pit, even if that meant being murdered by some lunatic who would probably eat whatever was left of me. At least I wouldn't die alone, trapped within the mud walls.

"Please help me," I called out, but my voice was even weaker.

I looked up at the top of the pit hoping Nora would appear with help, but she didn't. But someone was there. I could hear them. I blinked repeatedly, trying to bring them into focus.

A familiar face peeked down at me over the edge of the pit. Could it be?

"Ryan?" I said as I stood slowly, afraid he would disappear. But it couldn't be Ryan. That was impossible. Ryan was dead. Maybe I was dead too. "Can you help me?"

Ryan looked down at me and shook his head slowly. His glowing blue eyes turned black and then he sneered before he walked away.

"Ryan, I'm sorry! Please... please help me!" I begged, but he was gone.

I pressed my face into my arm, trying to force myself to wake up. This was a dream. It had to be.

"Ros."

The voice was soft... friendly. I knew the voice well. It hadn't been that long ago that I'd heard that voice in my ear every day.

I hugged myself as though I might fall apart. I didn't want to see him, but at the same time... I did. My fingernails dug into my palms as I looked up, "Dean!"

He tilted his head to the side and looked down at me with the same perfect smile I remembered. The Dean looking down at me was the Dean I remembered from those days in the shelter. He looked, well... happy.

231

"Oh Dean," I said crying so hard my whole body shook. "Please, help me Dean. I don't want to be down here anymore."

He didn't stop smiling even when he shook his head side to side. "It's not your time yet."

"It can be. Just take me with you! I miss you so much!" My body felt so cold. I wondered if death was coming for me once and for all.

He abruptly turned and looked over his shoulder. His smile faded before he walked away.

"Dean, no! Please! Please come back! Dean! Take me with you!" I said, my voice cracking with each word.

Then I was alone again. I couldn't take it anymore. Not that I had a choice. I just wanted to die. Any fight that I had in me, was gone.

I looked up at the sky to beg for death to come for me, but before I could ask, I was hit in the face with something wet. Then another in a different spot. Before I knew it, rain was pouring down.

I opened my mouth and let anything I could catch drip down my raw throat. Once I collected enough in my mouth, I swallowed the cool liquid, even though I knew I was only prolonging the inevitable. The thought of living longer in this hell made the tears flow just as fast as the rain did.

The sides of the pit smoothed as the rain washed down over them. Even if I would have had the energy, it would be impossible to even make another attempt at an escape.

The rain started coming down in sheets. It was a downpour and there wasn't anything I could do to escape the cold rain.

Water poured over the edges like little waterfalls and started to fill the bottom of the pit. The earth below was so damp it didn't soak up any of the water, it just held it. Before long the whole pit would be filled.

This could be my chance, depending on how much rain water would fill the hole.

If I could tread water long enough, maybe I could survive... that was, if I had the energy. And I didn't know if I should even bother trying.

The pit was filling fast. I was completely drenched and shivering. My body moved, but only barely. I was shaking uncontrollably and my teeth were chattering so loudly I was sure if anyone was out there, they could hear them.

"Help!" I shouted, my voice working only slightly better after having swallowed some of the rain. "Anyone... help! I'm down here!"

I was going to freeze to death before I even had a chance to try to tread water. If I could get to the top, I could pull myself over and try to find my way back to Penn. That is, if I was even still alive.

"Help!" I shouted again as loudly as I could, but the rain was so loud.

"Ros?" A voice shouted back. It sounded so far away. It didn't seem as though it could have been real. I probably only imagined it through the noisy rain. "Ros? Where are you?"

Was it real?

Was someone out there? Someone who knew my name... someone was looking for me.

"Help!" I shouted pressing my cold, purple-skinned fingers into the mud. I looked up, closing my eyes every time a drop hit my face. "I'm down here!"

I wasn't sure how much of what was happening was real and how much was a dream. For all I knew I was already dead.

The ice cold water was around my knees. My legs felt numb and I couldn't feel my feet. Hopefully the voice was real, because I didn't think I'd be able to communicate to my legs to tread water once the water was higher.

"Ros?" the voice called again, but this time, before I could respond, there was a shadowy figure standing above.

A light hit my eyes causing them to sting. My hand shot up instinctively to cover them.

"Jesus! Ros? Is that really you?" the voice said, and I peeked out from under my arm. The light was now focused on my body and I looked up towards the owner of the voice.

Standing at the top of the pit was Carter. His eyes were filled with concern, but he was wearing a huge smile. He was just as soaked as I was... but for all I knew, he wasn't real. He would probably disappear the same way Ryan and Dean had.

"Are you OK?"

"I'm freezing! But I think I'm alive."

He made a small laugh and then looked away, "You're alive. One second."

Carter disappeared from view and I started to panic.

"Carter! No! Come back!" I shouted,

staring up into the darkness.

Something splashed into the water next to me and I tried to move away from it. It was wiggling in the water like a snake, but I quickly realized what it was… a rope.

I looked back up and Carter was gesturing wildly, "Come on, grab it! I'll pull you up."

"How?" I said trying to hold on to the rope, but my fingers weren't working the way they should have. They were stiff and I couldn't get a good grip.

"Tie it around your waist. Can you do that?"

I took the rope and watched him more than I watched what I was doing. I was afraid that if I looked away, he'd vanish just as the others had.

"OK," I said after I checked the rope around my waist and twisted the end around my arm several times. "Ready."

After a few seconds, I felt the rope tighten. I pressed my hand against the wall to keep myself steady as I started to rise up and out of the water.

I slid against the muddy wall, but I was moving upwards and that's all that mattered. Tears streamed down my face along with the pouring rain. Even if I was dead, I was happy to be leaving the pit behind me.

When I was close enough to the top, I raised my arm. Carter grabbed it and pulled me up the rest of the way. I slid across the slick grass as he moved me further from my grave.

I felt the blades of dead grass under my fingers and I breathed heavily as I looked around at the tall trees surrounding us. "Is this real?" I said as I crawled closer to Carter. "Are you real?"

He smiled at me and pulled me into his arms. "I'm very real. And you're very cold. I need to get you back."

Carter quickly untied the rope and looped it around his shoulder. He helped me until he was sure I was steady on my feet. I nodded, and he clicked on the flashlight and took my hand as he led me away from the pit.

"You'll be OK. I'll get you back home and all warmed up," he said in a soothing voice.

"How did you know where to find me?" I said grabbing his arm trying to make sure he was real.

"Your friend," Carter said with a small laugh. "I almost killed her."

I shook my head. I didn't believe it. She'd found our place, told Carter, and he was able to rescue me. She hadn't left me for dead.

"Nora found you?" I asked.

"She did. She approached the house and when I saw her walking I lined up a shot, but when she dropped to her knees and then collapsed to the ground, I knew something wasn't quite right. I went out to check, gun pointed at her, and she mumbled your name."

"She did?"

Carter nodded as he ducked under a tree branch, "At first I thought I imagined it or that it was some kind of trick. But she was in sad shape… she was dying."

"Is she OK?" I asked in a squeaky voice.

"How far away are we?"

"She's fine, once I got her fed and warmed up she told me what happened. That back there... that was one of Penn's traps. He probably would have checked it on his way back," Carter said looking into my eyes. "He probably wouldn't have expected to find you in there."

I nodded, "He probably would have killed me."

"I don't know if he'd just shoot without checking first—"

"He would."

Carter nodded, "But I got to you first. Now let's keep moving, we're not that far."

"But I've been down there for two days... I don't think I can make it," I said almost too cold to feel the pain in my side.

"What? I don't think that can be," Carter said shaking his head. "You haven't been down there for two days. I helped Nora sometime this afternoon and walked straight here. It's only a few more miles."

I didn't know what was real and what wasn't anymore. The days and nights passing had felt so real. I had counted them. How could it have all been in my head?

"I'm not doing great, Carter. I saw them," I said wiping my nose with the back of my hand.

"Saw who?"

"Ryan... Dean... they're both dead and I saw them. They came to visit me," I said with a shiver.

Carter turned around as though he was

237

suddenly afraid we were being followed. "It was a dream… some kind of hallucination or something. You're going to be fine. You're with me now."

"If you're even real," I mumbled and started to drag my feet.

Carter pulled me along, practically carrying me. He was in a hurry to get me back inside our warm house.

Chapter twenty-six.

I tried to open my eyes but the stinging brightness forced me to close them again. Where were the mud walls? And why was it so bright?

"I think she's waking up," a soft voice whispered from somewhere. Then I heard footsteps.

I knew I was laying down when I tried to back away from the voice and couldn't move. There was nowhere to go... I couldn't make myself disappear.

After I rubbed my eyes, I started to remember. I remembered Carter saving me. He'd pulled me out of the pit and then we walked through the rain while I shivered. But that was all I could remember.

Was I back at our house? I couldn't remember walking towards the house, or coming inside. I couldn't remember much of anything after being pulled out of the pit.

"Ros?" Carter whispered, and I felt someone sit down on the bed next to me.

I placed my hand over my eyes to block out the bright light and tried to peek out between my fingers. The ceiling was the first thing I saw. I knew this ceiling... the one with the fan that didn't spin. I swallowed hard.

I was safe.

"Carter?" I said softly when I saw his hand resting on the bed next to me. Before he answered I put my hand down on top of his.

His other hand reached up and stroked my hair gently. I could feel the bits of dirt moving against my scalp each time he moved his fingers downward.

"You're home," he said as he lowered his head to look into my eyes. I saw his face between my fingers and I still wanted to doubt that he was real. It just didn't seem possible after everything I'd been through, that I was finally back inside our house.

"Where's Penn?" I said slowly pulling my hands away as I tried to force myself to sit up. I grimaced remembering the pain my side. It was bad again. Maybe even worse than before.

"He's out. He'll be back. He comes back frequently to check to see if you've returned," Carter said reaching forward to help adjust the pillows behind me.

"Where does he go?"

Carter tilted his head to the side and smiled, "He's looking anywhere and everywhere for you. He's canvasing the area methodically."

"Oh." It was all I could say. Of course, that's what he was doing.

"You know he'd never give up on you," Carter said moving closer to me and pulling me gently into his arms for a hug. I sighed as I felt his warmth soak through my body right into my still cold bones. "It's really good to have you back."

"It's good to be back... I never thought I'd

see you or this place again," I said looking around the room. Nora was sitting in a chair near the window watching us. "Nora!"

I tried to get up but my body wouldn't let me. Her arm moved slowly as she lifted her palm and smiled.

"You saved me," I said noticing that she had some of her color back. She still looked frail, but she looked better than she had the last time I'd seen her, which hadn't been that long ago.

"Your friend saved me," she said tipping her head towards Carter.

I didn't want to tell her that I had thought she abandoned me, although I probably owed her an apology. She sent me help, just like she said she would.

My smile faded when I met Carter's eyes again. I didn't want to tell him that she was from HOME. I wasn't exactly sure what I should or shouldn't tell him or Penn about Nora. My brain was still a jumbled mess of thoughts and I couldn't get them straightened out.

I could still remember Dean looking down at me through the rain. He looked so real. The memory made my whole body shiver.

"I should probably tell you what happened," I said pulling back from Carter slightly.

"Nora already told me."

"She did?" I looked in her direction, but she was staring out the window.

Carter glanced at Nora. "She told me everything about the facility, the dogs, the man... everything," he said rubbing my shoulder gently.

"Before the facility… a man… took me, he beat me. I would have died if it wasn't for the facility. They brought me there and saved my life. I wanted to get back here sooner, but I was too hurt. Still am," I said as a wave of memories washed over me. It was like an out-of-body experience seeing the man hitting me again like a movie playing in my mind. "My rib… the doctor there told me it was broken."

Carter scooted closer and pulled me into his arm. He pressed my head down onto his shoulder, "It's all over now. You're here. Penn and I won't let anything like that happen ever, ever again."

I started to feel tired. There was so much sleep I needed to catch up on and now that I was safe my body was craving the rest.

Carter said Nora told him everything, but I couldn't help but wonder how much detail she'd gone into. Had she told him that we suspected HOME was behind the facility? Did it even matter?

I tilted my head slightly to look at her. Had she confessed to Carter that I had found the tattoo? When our eyes finally met, I was the one to look away. I was pretty sure she wouldn't have told him, and I was also pretty sure she probably didn't want me to tell them either.

She said she'd moved on. Penn had moved on, maybe Nora could have too. Maybe HOME couldn't hold onto its people as easily as they thought they could once someone came to their senses. Not everyone fell for their mind control.

If I could accept that Penn could leave

242

HOME completely, then maybe I should also be willing to accept that someone else could too. What I did know was that I couldn't keep it from Penn or Carter. I would have to tell them what I had seen… but how?

My breathing slowed and I let my eyelids close. Resting against Carter's warm body made me feel safe, well, as safe as I could possibly feel.

When I woke, I was alone in the bedroom. I pushed myself up and peered out of the door looking for Carter or Nora. Somehow day had turned into night even though it had only felt as though I had been asleep for a few minutes.

"Carter?" I said, and he quickly dashed into the room.

"What is it?" he said looking around the room as if he expected something to be wrong.

Nora appeared outside of the door and looked in at us. She looked as though she had been sleeping and seemed confused, like she didn't know what was happening or how she could help.

"Nothing," I muttered, as I hugged myself and shivered. I looked back and forth between them and the dreadful feeling of aloneness drifted away. It felt as though maybe I had just had a bad dream, only I couldn't remember anything about it.

Carter felt my forehead as though he was worried I might be sick. Then he looked into my eyes, "You should eat. I'll get you something."

"You OK?" Nora asked with a yawn.

"Yeah, I'm fine."

She nodded and disappeared from view. I assumed she was going to go back to sleep.

243

Before Carter made it more than three steps away from the bedroom, there was a pounding on the front door. The knocking had a unique pattern.

He was back. It had to be him.

"Penn!" I whispered letting out a soft exhale filled with relief. I couldn't wait to see him.

Chapter twenty-seven.

Carter rushed to the door, his feet thudding hard against the floor as he moved across the room.

I grabbed my side and slowly walked out of the bedroom, stopping in the doorway. The thought of seeing Penn was sending all kinds of emotions through me... it was overwhelming.

He pushed back the curtain and nodded to a person who I assumed was Penn on the other side before undoing the lock. Carter pulled open the door and looked behind Penn to double check that he hadn't been followed. After Penn stepped inside, Carter closed the door and locked it.

"Ahhh," he said with a grunt and a shiver. "Cold out there." He dropped his backpack on the floor and spun around so he could hang up his coat.

I started taking small steps towards him. It didn't seem possible. I wasn't even sure if he was real. Was any of this real? It felt as though I rose slightly off of the ground and started floating towards Penn.

Carter was wearing a huge smile. Penn looked at him and scrunched up his face, "What's with you?"

He must have noticed movement out of the corner of his eye because he spun on his heel to face me. Penn froze in place and stared at me.

245

"What the…," he said glancing at Carter only for a brief second before turning back to look at me. He put his hand over his mouth but I could see the sides of his mouth rising. He was smiling. "Are you real? Is this real?" he asked turning towards Carter for a second. "Am I dreaming?"

He stared at me with a look in his eyes that made my breath stick in my throat. He took two large steps and lifted me off of my feet. Penn held my sore body tightly to his.

"I knew it!" he said putting me down and cupping my face with his ice-cold hands. "I knew you were still out there. I could feel it. I never gave up, isn't that right Carter?"

All I could do was smile at him and nod. The words got lost along the way. It was almost too much to take.

"If you don't say something, I'm not going to believe this is real. I probably died out there in the middle of nowhere and this is some kind of dream. The best dream, but still a dream," Penn said holding me so tightly I didn't think he'd ever let go. And I didn't want him to.

"It's really me," I choked out. He squeezed me so hard I let out a groan and my body weakened.

He moved his head back so he could see my face. I tried not to let the pain show, but I could tell he knew something wasn't right.

"What's wrong?" he said, his expression turning serious.

"Broken rib… I think. Or maybe just badly bruised. It was better, but since traveling back here it's bad again," I said not mentioning that falling into the pit hadn't helped.

He stepped away as though he was afraid he would break me. The worry showed in his eyes as they shifted towards my side.

"I'll be fine. I just need to let it heal," I said with a small, but hopefully reassuring, smile.

"Well, then sit, what are you doing up on your feet?" he said with an adorable smile.

Penn was helping me over to the sofa when Nora shifted in her chair ever so slightly. Penn's hand dropped off my back and in less than a second he had his gun pointed in her direction.

"Wait!" I said putting my hand on his arm. I tugged on his sleeve so he'd lower the gun, but he easily resisted my weak efforts. "She's with me! She helped me!"

I turned to look at Nora so that I could explain. Penn wasn't going to easily trust or accept her, and I figured she would probably understand, given the circumstances. But the words got lost when I turned my head and saw her standing there with her gun pointed right back at him.

I let go of Penn's arm and shook my head. Carter moved to Penn's other side, holding a shotgun down by his thigh.

"What's she doing here?" Penn said between clenched teeth.

"I told you she helped…." My words faded away as I looked back and forth between them. He wasn't being protective because I had brought a stranger into the house. It quickly became clear that this was something much more than that…

Penn recognized her. "Oh crap."

Chapter twenty-eight.

I told Penn everything. Everything that I could remember, and in as much detail as possible. Everything except the part about the tattoo. But he didn't drop his gun, or his guard... not even for a second.

When I finished talking, he blinked, but he didn't take his eyes off of her. He swallowed hard before breaking the silence.

"Do you remember me?" Penn asked.

Oh no.

Nora nodded, grinning at him with a sly smile and a slightly raised eyebrow, "I do."

"How long have you been away?" Penn said tightening his grip on his gun.

"Away?"

"From HOME. Don't lie... I'll know if you do," Penn said.

Nora laughed, "Oh please. The only way you'd know is if you were still working for them."

Penn's eyes shifted towards me for a split second as though he was worried about what I might think. Or if it might make me suspicious of him all over again.

"I left them a long time ago," he said shifting his weight, "but I have a feeling you already knew that."

"I left them too," Nora said. And since

Penn didn't pull the trigger, I wondered if he believed her.

"When?"

She shook her head, "I don't remember… it was some time ago. I believe they are looking for me. Just as they are probably looking for you."

Penn nodded. His free hand tightened into a fist and then relaxed. He looked a little more nervous than usual and he didn't take his eyes off of her as though he was expecting something to happen. I knew without a doubt that he didn't believe a single word that came out of her mouth.

"Watch the window," Penn said and Carter instantly moved, standing behind the curtain and looking out. He alternated between the two big windows near the door to change his view, but I doubted he could see anything out there in the darkness.

Penn was probably afraid she'd brought them with, but I knew she hadn't. At least I was pretty sure she hadn't. We weren't apart except for the amount of time between the pit and Carter bringing me back to our place. Would she have been able to contact them? Would she even have wanted to contact them?

I didn't trust her. In fact, after I saw the tattoo I tried to leave her behind. We stayed together because she had the gun, and I'd never been out of her sight for long enough to get away. The only time I could have escaped was when she was sleeping, and I never believed I'd be able to make a run for it. After all, she was trained by HOME. If I would have tried again, I believed she

250

would have pulled the trigger.

Then she did something I hadn't really expected... she saved me. Nora had made her way to Carter and sent him for me. If she wanted me gone, or any of us dead, she could have just killed Carter, left me to die and waited for Penn to return. But maybe she didn't know if Penn would return, and maybe she, or HOME, didn't want us dead. Maybe they had another plan.

"Why do you think they are looking for you?" Penn asked.

"Because of the place," she said and glanced at me.

He kept his eyes on her and lowered his voice for only me to hear, "It's too risky having her here."

"I know... but she saved my life," I whispered. "If she wanted me dead she could have easily made that happen."

Penn cleared his throat, "Nora and I were in several training programs together back at HOME."

"He was their number one student," she said with a smirk that seemed to hold a tinge of jealousy. "I have to admit, when I first saw you, I wasn't sure... you look a little different from the last time I saw you."

"I cut my hair," he said.

"Yeah, that must be it," Nora said glancing at me. "She was with me in the facility. She knows I wasn't with HOME."

I nodded my head, "That's true. They dropped her into my room. She was weak... hadn't eaten, at least that's what she told me."

251

I could tell Penn wasn't going to back down. He was desperately trying to put all of the pieces together. She'd been in the facility with me, but I had no idea what the facility was. It could have been connected to HOME, in fact Nora had speculated as much herself.

"Want to know what I think?" Penn said stepping away from me so he could pace the floor.

Nora rolled her eyes, "Oh, why not?"

"I think you are here for me. Maybe all of us, I can't rule that out. But since you didn't take Ros right away, the only conclusion I can come to is that she wasn't enough. You, or they, wanted more." Penn said as he walked the floor stopping in front of me. "You weren't that far behind in our training. You were also quite skilled, but then after a while... I didn't see you around the base much. Where did you go?"

She shrugged and shifted her weight from one leg to the other. Nora nodded at her gun, "Can we put these down?"

"Hmm... you can if you want to," Penn said as he started to pace again. I looked over at him and saw the grin on his face. I didn't like it. "I'll ask again, where did you disappear to? Did they send you out on a job?"

"They just switched me into a different kind of program. I wasn't as special as you were," she said, her lip quivering ever so slightly. I was sure Penn had noticed it too. "They had a different plan for me, I guess. I wasn't cut out to be a spy."

"Ahh," Penn said with a small laugh. I wished I could read his mind... I wanted to know everything he was thinking.

She tilted her head slightly and lowered her gun with a soft sigh. "None of it matters. I've left HOME behind. I'm done with them."

Penn kept his gun glued to Nora, but he shifted his eyes towards me, "Did you see her with any communication devices? How often has she been alone?"

"No," I said shaking my head. I would have remembered seeing her with one of those things. "We were rarely apart. The only time I can think of was when she came here to find Carter after I'd fallen into the pit."

Penn didn't say anything, but he continued pacing. I knew he was going over all of the bits of information in his head. Carter was keeping his attention mostly on the window, but occasionally he'd look at Nora. Thankfully, no one had come barging in to kill us... yet.

"Before I saw her tattoo—"

"You saw her tattoo and still brought her here?" Penn said and I could feel the anger and frustration radiating out of his entire body.

"She said she was done with them...," I said, but quickly shook my head. "I didn't have a choice. She had the gun! I tried to get away, but she stopped me and then the dogs came."

"Jesus Christ, Ros, some details would have been nice," Penn said hitting his thigh with a closed fist.

"You already knew she was from HOME when you saw her," I said with a frown. I could feel my own anger rising.

"But I didn't know you knew… and still brought her here! It's OK. All right. Let me think."

I took a breath, "Before I figured out she was from HOME, she was dropped into my room at the facility. I guess it's possible that wasn't a coincidence."

It wouldn't be unlike HOME to intentionally place her with me so they could learn more about their new patients. When she found out I had somewhere to go on the outside, maybe they let us escape.

Sure, she killed someone when we escaped, but HOME wouldn't care about one casualty… at least I didn't think they would. It could have been just a case of that person being in the wrong place at the wrong time. Nora didn't have a choice, and she took her out in favor of finding out more.

I shook my head. It just couldn't be. It was possible, but was it likely?

"Well, it was really easy for us to escape. Almost like they were purposefully staying out of the way," I said, looking at Nora. I didn't need to tell Penn that HOME would do whatever it took if there was something they wanted.

I could tell by the look on Penn's face that he would never be able to believe she wasn't still working for HOME. But I knew he'd want something to prove his suspicions were right.

He lowered his gun and smiled. "You swear you've left them behind?"

"I swear," Nora said making a cross over her heart. She spun the gun on her finger and put her palms out. "I hate them. They killed my friends… they tried to kill me too."

Penn just nodded. It didn't seem as though he cared to hear any of the words she spoke. At least not the ones that weren't related to the questions he asked.

"So you guys just walked out of that place, huh? And you shot someone? Is that right?" Penn asked crossing his arms.

"She did. I saw it," I said.

"See!" she said in a strange, child-like voice.

Penn started taking careful steps towards Nora, he stretched out his hand to offer a handshake. When Nora smiled and reached out to accept, he grabbed her hand, spinning her around.

He had her arm twisted around her back pulling her tight against his torso. He couldn't see her face but I could.

There was something about the look on her face that had changed. Instead of looking afraid, she looked like she was trying to figure out her next move. A counterattack.

Penn watched me as I watched her. It was like he would know the truth by looking at her through my eyes. In the blink of an eye he had his other arm bent tightly around her neck. Her eyes were wide as she started grabbing at his arm, trying to pull it down to loosen his grip. But her one thin arm wasn't strong enough.

"Do they know where we are?" Penn said through clenched teeth, keeping his eyes on mine.

"How would I know?" she spat out the

255

words as though they were coated in dirt.

He grabbed her tighter, "Do they know where we are?"

"You're going to break my arm," she whined.

"Answer me!"

There was a long pause before she opened her mouth. A pause that made all of the suspicions I'd ever had come rushing back. "Please!" She begged.

She avoided my eyes but based on the expression on her face, she knew she was in trouble. Penn had been right to suspect her. What I couldn't figure out was why she had saved me? Why did she send Carter out looking for me?

I walked up to her and looked her in the watery eyes. I inhaled a calming breath through my nose and slowly exhaled between my lips. Then I don't know what happened, but I slapped her as hard as I could across the face.

Her head turned to the side from the force. She slowly raised her head back up to look at me. Her hair was hanging in her face, but I could still see the darkness that filled her eyes.

"If you're HOME, why did you help me escape? Why are you doing all of this?" I said trying to keep myself calm. I wanted to hit her again. "You could have kept me in that stupid facility forever!"

Nora stared at me. Her shoulders rising and falling quickly with each breath. She looked as me as though she wanted to kill me, but then her shoulders slumped down.

"You got yourself into this mess because you failed the test. You were so eager to leave. They knew there was no way you would ever be convert. And then you said you knew somewhere we could go," Nora said. She sneered at me, "They wanted to know who was out there. Who you knew. Who you were desperate to get back to."

I looked at Penn as I started backing away from them. The guilt of having taken her back to our home was starting to fill me from head to toe. This was all my fault. How had I let this all happen?

"They thought you were resistance. That you'd lead me right to one of their camps. If there are even any of them left," she said looking at me as though she was trying to send some of the darkness from her eyes into mine. "What they didn't know was who you'd really lead me to."

I sucked in a sharp breath that stabbed my lungs and squeezed my rib. My tongue felt like sandpaper in my mouth as I turned to look at Penn. What had I done?

How long did we have before HOME came for us? For Penn? Penn's blood would be on my hands.

I should have killed her when I had the chance.

Chapter twenty-nine.

I tried to replay every moment with Nora over in my head. Had she communicated with them? I couldn't be sure that she hadn't.

She was trained by HOME the same as Penn had been, if she needed to communicate with HOME, she would have found a way. Unless, maybe, I was overestimating her.

"But when we left... you killed that girl. I saw you...," I said in a soft voice as the memory played in my mind.

"Did I?" she asked with a smirk. She was trying to make me question what I had seen happen with my own eyes. It seemed as though she wanted me to doubt myself.

"What was the purpose of the facility? Why was I there?" I said glancing around the room as though I was afraid someone would jump out and grab me.

"It's probably some kind of training center, or for recruiting... am I right?" Penn asked.

Nora didn't answer with words but I could tell Penn was right, or very close to being right, based on a small twitch near the corner of her eye. HOME was everywhere.

I pinched my eyes together hoping to force myself to wake up from this bad dream, but when I opened them again, everything was the same. While I wasn't trapped in the pit anymore, I was still trapped.

"I don't understand any of this." I shook my head as I pressed my fingers into my temples.

"Did HOME target her specifically?" Penn asked but again Nora was silent.

I combed my fingers through my hair, "I don't think they knew me. They didn't question me and it didn't seem like they treated me any differently than any of the other girls. Oh! And there were only girls in the facility, at least that I saw... and there was a nursery."

"Dammit!" Penn said his arms wrapping around her neck so tightly the veins bulged out of his arm. "They're growing an army?"

"Each girl there had a roommate... I think. They probably planted a spy with each one of us. To learn more about us, and to gauge our willingness to stay" I said, but I was making a guess. It was too hard to put the puzzle together when I was missing so many pieces. My speculations seemed plausible, but I didn't think Nora would confirm my suspicions.

Penn chuckled and then started dragging Nora across the floor. She struggled against him but Penn was stronger. Nora was still weak from not having enough food.

"Stop! Let me go!" Nora said trying to kick her feet up at him. But it was like he could predict her every move.

He pulled his gun out and pressed it hard against her skull. Strands of hair covered her face,

259

but I could still see her panicked expression.

"Why? You're not talking... I have no use for you," Penn said practically spitting out the words. "Are you going to talk? Are you going to tell us something about the facility?"

The room was completely silent. When she shook her head side to side, I was sure I heard it move.

Penn nodded to Carter who looked out both windows before opening the front door. He stepped outside with his gun drawn, shifting around as he checked to make sure the coast was clear.

"What are you going to do?" I shouted after them, as Penn dragged Nora outside. If he heard me... he ignored me. Penn slammed the door shut and all was quiet except for my breathing. "Penn!"

I ran up to the door clutching my side, and hit it with my closed fist. It wasn't like I needed Penn to tell me what they were going to do. I already knew.

"Arrrrh!" I shouted at the door before I pressed my forehead into it. There wasn't anything I could do but wait for Penn to clean up my mess. How did I let this happen?

I started back towards the sofa, dragging each foot as though it weighed twenty pounds. When I heard the gunshot, my whole body jerked. I paused for a second to breathe, but then I forced my feet to keep moving forward.

Penn told her he'd be able to tell if she was lying. He must have seen something... somehow he must have known. It was probably all part of his training.

He did what had to be done. Knowing she was part of HOME, there was no way we could let her leave alive. What choice did any of us have?

The only choice we had in the matter was who would take care of the situation. I knew it had to be done, but it didn't have to be done by Penn. It should have been my job. I was the one that screwed up, but Penn took matters into his own hands. He took care of me... watched over me, just as he'd always done.

I sat down on the sofa and waited.

Chapter thirty.

If I had to guess, it was probably about an hour later when the door opened. Penn stepped aside so Carter could enter before he took a final look into the darkness.

He closed the door and locked it. I watched him as he walked past me… my stomach sank when he didn't even glance in my direction.

"Penn," I murmured, but he kept walking. He went into the bedroom and closed the door softly.

I looked up at Carter. There wasn't anything I could do to stop the tears from filling my eyes. I wasn't sure if they were tears of sadness, frustration, anger, or something else, but they were there and I couldn't make them go away.

"It's OK," Carter said with a soft smile.

"I screwed up," I said covering my mouth with my fingertips.

"Everything is going to be OK. He's just changing his clothes. He got a little wet when we…."

"When you?"

"Threw her into the lake," He said quietly.

I nodded. I swallowed hard thinking about Nora's body drifting in the lake. I knew why it had to be done, but I wasn't going to be happy about it. It was all still my fault that it had to happen.

When I was out there with her, I felt like I didn't have a choice but to stay with her. Maybe on some level there was part of me that didn't want to be left alone. My thoughts hadn't been clear because all I could think about was getting back to Penn and Carter. I should have taken matters into my own hands when I had the chance, but I had been too weak.

Penn came out of the bedroom and looked at me before he lowered his head. He sat down next to me and leaned back, resting his head against the back of the sofa. I waited, but he didn't say anything and started picking at his fingernail.

"I'm so sorry, Penn," I said turning towards him as much as my side would allow. Even though he didn't need to, Carter walked into the kitchen in an attempt to give us a little privacy.

"It's not your fault," Penn said taking my hand into his. "It's really not."

I looked away from him, "What if she talked to them? They could be on their way right now."

"I don't think she had a chance."

"How can you be sure?"

"I can't," he said shaking his head. Penn looked down at our hands, "If she thought they were coming, I think she would have tried harder to stay alive, knowing her saviors were on their way. But she didn't try. She didn't give us a damn thing."

I frowned, "She could have talked to them after she left me. She could have talked to them after Carter left her alone to come looking for me."

263

"There are no communication devices on this property. I suppose she could have found something along the way, but I'm not sure. If she was starving she probably just came here first," Penn said looking as though he was trying to convince himself that what he was saying had to be true.

I didn't want to leave. This was our home. This was where I was supposed to be. I felt it so strongly, and since Penn wasn't packing our things and chasing us out of the door, I had to think maybe he felt it too.

"All we can really do is hope that I'm right. Or go out and start looking for a new place." He looked at Carter as he moved around in the kitchen. Penn leaned towards me and lightly touched my chin with his fingertip. He turned me so I had to look into his eyes. "I'm willing to bet my life she didn't tell them, but if you want to go... we'll go. Whatever you want."

I shook my head, "No. I want to stay. If they come... well, then we will fight."

Penn nodded and glanced at Carter who clearly had been listening in on our conversation. He grinned and leaned back against the counter. It almost looked as though he was daring HOME to come.

If they came, they'd win. No question about it. They had numbers we didn't have. But I was sick of running. If Penn didn't think they were on their way, then I believed him, and if he just happened to be wrong... then we'd stand our ground and fight.

264

That night, Penn and I lay in bed together, our shoulders touching. I liked feeling him there... knowing he was next to me.

The floorboards in the living room creaked and I knew Carter wasn't sleeping. If he was trying to, he was failing miserably. I was pretty sure if I peeked out of the bedroom door, I would see him walking to the windows, checking them every so often to make sure HOME wasn't approaching.

Penn's breathing gave away the fact that he wasn't sleeping either. He was probably worried that he was wrong and that HOME would come bursting through the door and windows at any moment.

"Are you awake?" I whispered even though I knew he was.

"Yeah."

I swallowed hard, "I'm scared."

Penn turned to face me. His eyes glowing in the dim lighting. "Ros, we're survivors. We've been to hell and back and we are still here to talk about it. Maybe it's luck, I don't know, but when I'm with you, I feel like we can't lose."

"Our time is just around the corner," I whispered into the darkness.

"We'll take it one day at a time. If HOME doesn't know we are out here, well, then we have a lot of days to work with. I will protect you until the day I die," Penn said with a soft breath. "I promise."

I didn't know what to say. There was no doubt in my mind that Penn meant his words. If he made a promise, he would keep it.

Penn and Carter were all I had left, and I didn't want to lose either of them. If we worked together, who knows how long we could survive in this house? As long as HOME stayed away.

Of course, we'd never be able to beat everything HOME was, they were too big and too powerful. They grew with each passing day. Eventually they'd take over everything, but how long would that take? Maybe it would take a lifetime.

I wanted to find out.

My whole body jumped when Carter knocked on the frame of the bedroom door. He looked back and forth between us. I couldn't read his expression.

"What is it?" Penn asked as he pushed himself up. "Is it HOME? Are they here?"

"No," Carter said shaking his head, but he gestured towards the window. "It's snowing. Not just flurries. It's really snowing."

Penn jumped up off of the bed and looked out the window. I followed behind, wrapping my arms around myself as if I could feel the cold outside air.

It was really coming down. Thick, heavy flakes landed on the window and stuck for several seconds before starting to slowly melt into a tiny droplet of water.

"Do we have enough wood? Of course we don't! We're going to need more wood," Penn said looking as though he was going to go out and start gathering more in the middle of the night… in a snowstorm.

266

"We should have enough," Carter said with his hands on his hips.

"Food? Water? It's not enough! Dammit, we should have been more prepared!"

Carter put his hand on Penn's shoulder, "We are prepared for this. We knew this would happen."

"Ugh!" Penn said stepping away from Carter so he could pace the bedroom floor. "We should have been *more* prepared."

Penn stopped in front of the window, watching the flakes fall down. Winter wouldn't slow HOME. We couldn't let it slow us either.

A smile stretched across my face so wide Penn couldn't help but notice. He looked at me with a raised eyebrow.

"What?" he said trying not to return a smile.

"We can do this. I know we can. Together. We're going to be OK. Right Carter?"

"Of course we will," he said with an equally large grin.

I looked out the bedroom window, smiling at the snow. My confidence grew with each snowflake that covered the ground.

"Yeah, we can do this," I said looking back and forth between Carter and Penn. Carter's smile was just as confident, but Penn's expression was serious. He looked at Carter and then me and shook his head like we'd lost our minds.

I turned back towards the window and took in a deep breath. It was strange after everything I'd been through, but I stood there watching the snow fall, feeling braver and stronger than ever before.

I was ready. Whatever this new life had to

throw at me next, I was ready. I knew I could do whatever it would take to survive.

***

Books By Kellee L. Greene

Ravaged Land Series

Ravaged Land -Book 1
Finding Home - Book 2
Crashing Down - Book 3
Running Away - Book 4
Escaping Fear - Book 5
Book 6 - Spring/Summer 2017

The Landing Series

The Landing - Book 1
The Aftermath - Book 2

About the Author

Kellee L. Greene is a stay-at-home-mom to two super awesome and wonderfully sassy children. She loves to read, draw and spend time with her family when she's not writing. Writing and having people read her books has been a long time dream of hers and she's excited to write more. Her favorites genres are Fantasy and Sci-fi. Kellee lives in Wisconsin with her husband, two kids and two cats.

Coming Soon

Kellee is currently working on several new projects, including another series. Please follow Kellee L. Greene on Facebook to be one of the first to hear about what's new.

www.facebook.com/kelleelgreene

Mailing List

Sign up for Kellee L. Greene's newsletter for new releases, sales, cover reveals and more!

http://eepurl.com/bJLmrL

Thank you for reading my novel.

If you liked this story, there are two things you can do to help. The first is to spread the word! Tell family and friends, share it on Facebook, Twitter, Goodreads and similar sites, or buy it as a gift for someone you think might enjoy it.

The second thing you can do to help, is to leave a review.

Reviews are important, especially to new writers, like me, because it's hard to get noticed among all the other great authors. There are so many writers trying to get noticed, and great reviews help new writers stand out from the crowd.

Even if you don't like leaving reviews or don't have time, I'm still extremely happy and excited you read my book. That means the world to me and I thank you from the bottom of my heart.

But if you do have a few minutes, leaving a review will help me build an audience, get noticed, and could make a huge impact on my writing career. It doesn't need to be a long review, a short honest review is just as helpful.

Again, a huge thank you for reading my novel.

~Kellee L. Greene~

Made in the USA
Monee, IL
24 November 2024

71085856R00154